MATHESON'S LEGACY

•

James Clay

AVALON BOOKS
NEW YORK

Published by Thomas Bouregy & Co., Inc.
160 Madison Avenue, New York, NY 10016

Library of Congress Cataloging-in-Publication Data

Clay, James.
  Matheson's legacy / James Clay.
     p. cm.
  ISBN 978-0-8034-9941-6 (acid-free paper)   1. Sheriffs—
Fiction.   2. Arizona—Fiction.   I. Title.

  PS3603.L387M38   2009
  813'.6—dc22   2008031625

PRINTED IN THE UNITED STATES OF AMERICA
ON ACID-FREE PAPER
BY HADDON CRAFTSMEN, BLOOMSBURG, PENNSYLVANIA

For Virginia and Doug, with hope
that they will not be too embarrassed.

Chapter One

"They fired at us from right inside that bar, Sheriff!" Naomi Willis pointed at the Roman Holiday Saloon. Her speech was broken as she gasped for air. She had run from the saloon to the sheriff's office and was now returning with the lawman. "All we were doing was practicing our right to condemn the devil's own brew."

On the boardwalk in front of the saloon were three well-dressed ladies with faces that were ashen. One was holding a sign proclaiming: THERE ARE NO SALOONS IN HEAVEN. When they saw Naomi and the sheriff, they became emboldened and began to sing again.

"When the trumpet of the Lord shall sound, and time shall be no more, And the morning breaks, eternal bright and fair . . ."

Sheriff Boyd Matheson sighed inwardly. The ladies were obviously shaken, and being shot at had not helped them to sing on key.

1

"Do your duty, Sheriff!" Naomi shouted. She was a dark-haired woman with a pinched, sullen-looking face. "We need to make Gradyville the kind of town where a woman can march into a saloon and smash the liquor bottles without fear of being injured or insulted by some drunken lout!"

"You didn't try anything like that, did you, Miss Willis?"

"No! We were only standing outside the saloon doors singing hymns."

Matheson stifled a laugh. If they had tried to destroy property, he could have thrown the temperance ladies in jail. Of course, they probably would have started singing in their cell. That would have made the day pretty long.

"Sheriff, we have every right to—"

"Yes, you do, Miss Willis. I'll take care of it."

The lawman stepped hastily onto the boardwalk and touched two fingers to his hat as he passed the singing ladies, who were now being rejoined by Naomi.

"When the saved of earth shall gather over on the other shore . . ."

Inside the saloon, half a dozen men were angrily watching the spectacle outside; one of them was Walter Jarrett, the owner of the Roman Holiday. Jarrett was a middle-aged, medium-sized man with brown, curly hair and a well-tended mustache. As he spoke, he puffed on a cigar lodged in the right side of his mouth. "Those crazy women are driving away my customers." Jarrett didn't bother with a greeting. "I've heard cat fights that sounded better."

". . . and the roll is called up yonder, I'll be there."

"Mr. Jarrett, did you or any of your customers take a shot at the ladies?"

"I offered to buy one of them a shot of whiskey!" The shout came from Ollie Jones, a short, gray-bearded gent who sat alone at one of the tables. Matheson couldn't remember ever seeing Ollie anyplace else except in a bar.

"Dencel Hayes fired over their heads." Walter Jarrett pointed his right thumb at a tall, stocky young man who stood beside him.

"They had it comin'," Dencel proclaimed. "If those hens get their way, it'll be against the law for a man to have a drink." He raised his voice at the women on the boardwalk. "Stop cawin', ya old crows!"

Dencel Hayes had not been in trouble before, Matheson reflected. He worked at a ranch outside of town.

"I want everyone here to listen to what I have to say." Matheson tried to keep the frustration out of his voice.

"When the roll is called up yon–der . . ."

"Speak up, Sheriff!" Ollie Jones shouted. "Can't hear ya over all that fool singin'."

Matheson raised his voice. "I want all of you to leave those ladies alone! After a while, they'll go away."

"When liquor is forsaken, and we give a kick to Satan, and the roll is called up yonder, I'll be there."

"They made that part up!" Dencel Hayes sounded genuinely offended. "They changed the words of a church song. That's indecent, and I'm gonna tell 'em so." The young man charged toward the saloon doors.

Matheson grabbed his left arm. "Hold on—"

Dencel used his free arm to take a strong but wild swing at the sheriff. Matheson tripped the boy and sent him sprawling to the floor. Hayes quickly scrambled to his feet and charged at Matheson.

Dencel needed to be stopped fast before he forced the lawman to really hurt him. Matheson delivered a haymaker against the left side of the young man's head. Once again Dencel plunged to the floor, and this time Matheson was confident that he wouldn't come up fighting.

As Matheson stooped over to help the boy up, Walter Jarrett's cigar was suddenly a few inches from his face. "You shouldn't have done that, Sheriff." Jarret waved the cigar back and forth as he talked. "Dencel was only trying to defend the sacred hymns of the church."

Matherson grimaced at Jarrett's sudden interest in spiritual matters as he helped Dencel to his feet. "Am I goin' to jail, Sheriff?"

Boyd Matheson's chest tightened. Without intending to, he had inhaled a good amount of Jarrett's cigar smoke. He cleared his throat before talking. "Not if you leave town—now. Stay on the ranch for a couple of days."

The temperance ladies were starting in on "Amazing Grace" as the lawman led Dencel Hayes out of the saloon. Hayes' steps were slow and cautious.

"Stay away from Beelzebub's bottles, young man!" Naomi shouted at Dencel as Matheson helped him onto his horse, which was tied to the hitching rail outside the saloon. "That way you won't disgrace yourself in front of the whole town!"

"I ain't drunk, jus' beat up!" Dencel shouted defensively before he pulled on his horse's bridle and began a slow ride back to his workplace.

"I think we can quit now," Naomi said to her companions. "We've saved one soul from perdition. Not a bad day's work."

The other three ladies looked at the departing cowboy. They obviously didn't share Naomi's optimism regarding Dencel's soul, but after being mocked and shot at, they were more than pleased to call it quits.

Matheson nodded at the ladies, wished them a good day, and then proceeded on his round, or pretended to. Confident that no one was watching him, the lawman retreated into an alley between a gun shop and a hardware store, where he surrendered to the deep cough that had been inside him since he inhaled the cigar smoke.

He tried not to make much noise, which only seemed to make his coughing more convulsive and painful. As the convulsions ceased, he leaned against the wall of the gun shop and fought for breath. The sheriff's breathing was starting to return to normal when he heard the gunshots.

Matheson ran from the alley and looked down the street. A rapidly expanding dust cloud was moving at him from the direction of the bank. The sound of gunshots pierced the low rumble of running horses. From the edge of the cloud, the lawman saw a red flame flare in his direction. He returned fire, and a man's panicked scream became a childlike cry as a gunman plunged downward into a barrage of heavy hoofbeats.

Horses pranced about wildly as the outlaws tried not

to stampede over their comrade. They fired at the lawman while trying to regain control of their steeds. Concern for the wounded bank robber was short lived. The
remaining four outlaws spurred their horses for a fast
gallop out of town, leaving a trampled body in the middle of the street.

Boyd Matheson stumbled and fell.

Chapter Two

Four horses galloped quickly from the town of Gradyville, Arizona, their riders young and scared. In the saddlebags of the lead rider was over fifteen thousand dollars.

A few miles outside of town, they stopped beside a stream to refresh their horses. "Can't stay here long." Russ Cavanaugh looked behind him as he dismounted. "They've got a posse formed by now."

"Boy, ain't you the smart one." Steve Gibbs' face and voice were drenched in anger.

"What's yer point, Gibbs?" Cavanaugh knew he had to be tough. All of the men were now off their horses. Two of the gang were standing behind Russ, anxiously watching the exchange between their boss and Steve Gibbs.

"I mean, the judge tol' us to scout out some good locations to rob. We wasn't supposed to pull no bank job, just report back."

"The judge put me in charge!" Russ Cavanaugh suddenly realized that, like everyone else, he called his father "the judge." Had he, as a child, called him Pop or Father? He couldn't remember.

"Yeah, well, he ain't puttin' you in charge of nothin' again. You shoulda checked with the judge first, but, no, you had to be the big man. Well, big man, you got scared and shot that bank clerk for no reason at all. Then one of our own men got killed while we rode out. I tol' you the sheriff of that town, Boyd Matheson, has got a reputation for bein' tough."

"Yeah, well, Matheson is dead now. I put a bullet in him."

Gibbs spit on the ground in front of his boss, as if mocking the braggart's words. "Whatta you talkin' about? Matheson just fell while he was dodgin' bullets. He rolled up fast and got off another shot at us. You didn't even wing him! You couldn't hit a tin can that was three feet in front of you."

There was a sudden quiet except for the sound of horses sucking up water. Russ felt that horrible fear overcome him again. The fear he had when he saw the judge giving more and more power to one of the other members of the gang and passing him over for the important jobs. He couldn't let Gibbs best him.

Russ walked directly toward the man who had challenged him, not stopping until they were less than a foot apart. That was a mistake. Steve was the tallest of the four men, and Russ felt edgy looking up at him. "Gibbs, maybe you'd better quit this outfit right now."

"You can't—"

"Take your cut, and get out."

Gibbs looked startled. He had not expected this. "You mean it?"

"Sure." Cavanaugh pointed behind him. "The money is in my saddlebags. Take what ya have coming to ya. Of course, my horse has taken a few steps into the water. You might have to get your feet wet. Hope that don't cause ya no pain."

The two other bank robbers guffawed at the boss' humor. Steve Gibbs looked contemptuously at all of them. "We'll see how hard you're all laughin' when they put a noose around your necks."

Gibbs pushed his boss aside and stepped quickly toward Cavanaugh's horse. Russ drew his gun and fired once into Gibbs' back. The explosion caused the horses to erupt in frightened neighs, and the other two robbers ran into the water to grab the reins of the animals. Steve Gibbs turned toward his killer and received another bullet in the stomach. He fell to the ground without touching his gun.

Cavanaugh still held the six-shooter in his hand as he spoke. "Porter, Amos, you guys have any problems with doing what I say?"

"No, Russ," Porter replied nervously, "Like you said, the judge made you the boss." Amos nodded his head in agreement but said nothing. The horses began to calm.

"Should we bury . . ." Porter pointed at the corpse as his boss holstered his gun.

"Let the buzzards have him," Cavanaugh said.

"But the posse will trail us here, and—"

"I said, let the buzzards have him, Porter. The posse

won't be able to trail us anywhere." The boss smiled at his own presumed cleverness. "Help me break off some branches from these trees."

"But why?"

"Just do what you're told!"

The two men had turned toward the trees, when they heard hoofbeats pounding away from them. "Amos, come back here, you—" Cavanaugh pulled out his pistol and fired two shots at Amos, who was riding fast and bent over low on his steed.

"You missed him, Russ."

"I can see that! The yellow—ah, let him go. That will just make our cut a lot bigger."

Porter fidgeted nervously as his boss ejected the empty cartridges from his gun and pushed in new ones. "The judge will sure be proud o' us. I mean, coming back with all this money."

Cavanaugh caught the uncertainty in his accomplice's voice. "The judge will be just fine with it. But first we're going to stop by and visit an old friend of mine."

Sheriff Boyd Matheson stood up after examining the corpse on the trail. "He hasn't been dead much more than an hour."

"I guess our bank robbers got into a bit of a spat." Deputy Clay Adams was looking carefully at the ground. "One of them rode off by himself, and he left pretty fast."

Matheson smiled bitterly as he also looked at the ground near Steve Gibbs' body. "At least one of the gang can read."

"How do you know that?" the deputy asked. The two lawmen were by themselves. Matheson had not gathered up a posse. From the sheriff's experience, a posse quickly became unreliable once the initial outrage and excitement wore off.

"Look at those marks on the ground." Matheson nodded his head downward. "They're moving northeast, the opposite direction of the tracks you were looking at."

"Looks like they're dragging something."

"That's exactly what they're doing." Matheson looked a touch embarrassed. "I read dime novels now and again."

Adams shrugged. "Me too. Some of them are pretty good."

"Yeah, and some of them are pretty bad. Like one I read lately, where an outlaw tied up a bunch of branches and dragged them behind him to cover his tracks."

"But that would just leave—" Adams laughed out loud. "Following those drag marks will be easier than following any tracks."

Matheson mounted his roan. "Let's get to it."

"Should we bury the body first?"

"A whole town is relying on us to get their money back. We'll have to return and bury that outlaw later." Matheson spotted two coyotes waiting patiently from behind the trees. "That is, if there's anything left to bury."

"I don't understand, boss." Porter untied the branches that he had been pulling behind his horse and returned his rope to his saddle.

"We've lost the posse by now." Russ Cavanaugh was

following the same procedure, a procedure that he had ordered. "I don't want any questions from Zack Johnstone or his father. Their spread is close by."

"How long have you known Zack?"

"We was kids together in Yuma, best friends until three years ago when Zack's uncle died. His aunt had been dead for years."

"So, Zack's pap came here to take charge of the ranch?"

"Yeah, and from what folks say, it's a big spread."

Gunshots sounded from nearby.

Zack Johnstone looked down at the smoking gun in his right hand, then shifted his gaze back to the row of cans. "I hit two out of four," he mumbled to himself. "That's a long way from being Wyatt Earp."

Zack wanted to be Wyatt Earp. He had read somewhere that Earp initially became a lawman because he hated ranching. "Know how he feels," Zack continued to mumble. "I'd be happy if I never saw another cow except on a plate."

The sound of approaching horses roused him from his private thoughts. Two riders were coming down a steep hill, and one of them was waving at him. Zack cautiously holstered his gun.

As the riders drew close, Zack didn't recognize either one of them. But he did recognize the voice that shouted out, "Good thing you're practicing your draw, Zack. Any day now they'll find out it was you and me that put that goat inside the schoolroom."

"Russ!" Zack shouted back. "Russ Cavanaugh!"

Cavanaugh dismounted, and the two boyhood companions shook hands and began to swap information about their families and mutual friends. Zack was happy to see his pal, but a sense of unease began to itch inside him. There had been more than a few changes in his chum since their school days.

Russ Cavanaugh now looked like drawings Zack had seen of Buffalo Bill. Cavanaugh's sandy hair came down to his shoulders, and a well-tended beard covered his cheeks and came to a point under his chin. All that might look good on Buffalo Bill, Zack thought, but Russ looked like a boy dressing up in his father's clothes.

Cavanaugh had briefly introduced the man riding with him as Porter. Porter's face was covered by a bushy mustache and a look of confusion. Zack had seen that look on other men. They were men who were always waiting for someone else to tell them what to do.

"So, what brings you to this neck of the woods?" Zack asked the question for the second time. First time around, Russ had brushed it aside for more recollections of childhood pranks.

"Well, Zack, you've probably been hearing stories about the judge—some good, some not so good."

"Me and Pa are hoping that those bad stories aren't true."

"They're not." Cavanaugh's smile widened as he continued to speak. "The judge has seen a lot of bad things in his day, and now he's trying to even the score—get back at the crooks who got away with it. Crooks like Elroy Vaughn."

"Vaughn, the banker?"

"Yeah. Years ago Vaughn cheated a couple out of a thousand dollars. Oh, it was all legal and everything—nothing the judge could do about it. The man Vaughn cheated is dead now, and the widow could sure use the money, so Porter and me just made us a little withdrawal—"

"You robbed the bank!"

Cavanaugh placed a hand on the right shoulder of his friend. "We only took a thousand dollars. That's not much for a bank, but it'll mean a whole lot to that widow."

"Reckon so . . ."

Cavanaugh started speaking at a faster clip, taking advantage of his friend's uncertainty. "We need a little help from you. We lost the posse, but they'll probably keep looking for us until sundown. Maybe you could hide us out somewheres till dark, then bring us some fresh horses and maybe some grub. We got us a lot of riding to do."

Zack was silent. Russ Cavanaugh remembered that his boyhood friend had always been uneasy over the fact that his family was wealthy. "It won't be much trouble for you, and that widow lady will mightily appreciate it."

Johnstone forced a smile to his face; he knew that he was doing wrong, but for some reason be couldn't turn his friend down. "Well, there is a line shack not being used right now. . . ."

Ezra Johnstone's smile was genuine. "Boyd, Clay, good to have you here! Come on in."

As the two lawmen stepped inside the ranch house, Boyd noticed that Ezra had dropped some weight since his wife's death four months ago. But he was still a strong-looking man with iron gray hair and a face lined by years in the hot sun.

"I hope you two can stay for supper."

"Afraid not, Ezra. We're here on business." As Matheson spoke, Zack came through the front door, and there were the usual quick hellos.

"The sheriff and his deputy are here on business, Zack." Ezra spoke in a humorous manner. "I haven't found out who they plan to arrest—you or me."

There was a moment of good-natured laughter. Then Matheson turned serious. "The bank was held up today. The robbers killed Rollie Jensen."

"No! That can't be!" Zack's voice was a shout. He slapped a hand against his wide forehead, then ran it over his brown hair.

Ezra placed a hand on his son's right shoulder as Russ Cavanaugh had done less than an hour before. Zack felt queasy.

"Rollie was a fine man, Sheriff. You must think the snakes who did it are in this area."

"Yeah, I do, Ezra. The crooks seem to have turned on one another. One of them is dead—shot in the back. Another seems to have broken rank. We think the other two are still riding together with the money—around fifteen thousand."

Ezra misinterpreted his son's trembling as outrage. "Zack and I will do whatever we can. You can deputize every ranch hand we've got, for that matter!"

"Appreciate it," Matheson said, "but for now just keep your eyes open." The sheriff eyed the younger Johnstone. "Seen anything unusual today?"

"No, Sheriff. Nothing at all."

The two lawmen were perched, prone, on top of a small hill that sat about a quarter mile to the east of the Johnstone ranch house. "We've got a bright moon tonight—that'll help us." Matheson lowered the field glasses he had trained on the house.

"Don't claim to know Zack very well," Clay Adams said, "but he sure did look jittery. He almost jumped out of his boots when you told them that Rollie Jensen was killed."

"We tracked the two riders to this ranch. There doesn't seem to be a trail leaving here." Matheson continued to keep his eyes fixed on the ranch house. Both lawmen were lying on the ground. "I think Zack is involved somehow. You're right—he's plenty nervous. I think he'll make a move tonight. When he does, we'll follow him."

Boyd Matheson was feeling a bit nervous himself. He rarely had more than one bad coughing spell in a day, but tonight, one loud hack could alert Zack that he was being watched.

Adams noticed his boss' unease. "Anything wrong?"

"No, just a little hungry, that's all. Think I'll get some jerky from my saddle. We may be here a spell."

Zack stood outside his father's door and listened carefully. He couldn't hear anything. His pa never snored. He was a hardworking man who slept soundly. On this night, Zack hadn't slept at all.

Russ Cavanaugh couldn't be a killer, Zack thought. A man can't change that much.

As he slipped outside and stepped lightly toward the barn, Zack recalled some worrisome memories. Both he and Russ had been mischievous boys, but there had often been a dangerous, hurtful quality to Russ' pranks. Sometimes Zack had been able to talk Russ out of those pranks, sometimes not. Like the time Russ suddenly pushed Billy Stanton off a roof the three boys had climbed up onto. Billy ended up with a broken arm. It could have been a lot worse.

The barn door didn't creak at all as Zack opened it. The young man picked up three bridles and his saddle. He didn't know how he would explain the absence of two horses to his father. Of course, he could replace them with the horses Russ and Porter would leave behind, but his pa would notice the change. Zack had not really thought the matter through.

Walking briskly toward the corral, the young man realized that there were a lot of things he hadn't thought through.

As the line shack came into view, Zack noticed that there were no horses tied up outside. Russ must have them hidden in a nearby grove of trees. Again, Zack Johstone's body trembled as he wondered if he was becoming an accomplice to murder.

He had just started to tie the horses to a hitch rail outside the cabin, when the door opened, and a smiling Russ

Cavanaugh stood in the doorway. "Obliged, amigo," Cavanaugh said in a loud whisper. "The horses look good, but, say, didn't ya bring us any chow?"

Zack pushed Cavanaugh into the shack and closed the door. "Why didn't you tell me that you killed Rollie Jensen?"

Cavanaugh shrugged and smiled as if explaining away a practical joke that had gone bad. "We didn't mean to kill anyone. But that clerk pulled a gun on us. Gave us no choice, the fool. We were only taking a thousand dollars."

"The sheriff says you took it all—fifteen thousand!"

"That's a lie!"

"Boyd Matheson is no liar."

Russ Cavanaugh shifted his gaze to Porter, whose face was twitching. The man was wound tight, waiting for Russ to signal him to go for his gun. Maybe Zack Johnstone would have to be killed, but Russ hoped not. For years Cavanaugh had played Zack for a fool to get what he wanted. He hoped that situation could continue.

Russ decided on a different approach. "Look, the sheriff may be an honest man, but Elroy Vaughn is a crook, and a smart crook to boot. He probably told that sheriff friend of yours that all the money got cleaned out of the bank. Tell the lawdog to check the house of that banker. I bet there's fourteen thousand dollars hidden away in some closet."

A loud shout came from outside. "This cabin is surrounded. Throw out your guns, and come out, hands high!"

Cavanaugh quickly glanced at the shack's only window, which was located on the back wall. He couldn't see anyone outside, but, of course, that meant little. He angrily grabbed the front of Zack's shirt. "Did you bring the law here?"

"No, Russ, honest. They came to the ranch this afternoon, but I told them nothing."

"Bet you were more nervous than the time you watched me strangle a cat. You never were tough, Zack, just the spoiled son of a rich man."

"Listen . . ."

"You do the listening. You got us into this mess. You're going to help us get out. How many lawdogs are there?"

"Two. That's how many came to the ranch. Matheson and his deputy."

"If they hadn't formed a posse by then, they probably didn't form one at all." Cavanaugh was speaking partially to himself. "Look, rich boy, you're going to do exactly what I tell you."

Boyd Matheson crouched behind a boulder and eyed the line shack that was less than ten yards away. Clay Adams was covering the back, in case the robbers tried to use the shack's only window.

A gun was tossed out the front door, and Zack Johnstone walked outside holding his hands up. "I need to talk with you, Sheriff."

"Where are the others?" Gun in hand, Matheson stepped from behind the rock and approached the young man who was walking steadily toward him.

"They want to surrender, but first they need to hear some promises from you."

"What kind of promises?"

"They want to know that you'll promise them a fair trial, with—"

Zack's arm moved like a whip, delivering a hard blow to Matheson's jaw. The lawman hit the ground, still holding on to his gun.

"Run!" the young man shouted. On his back, the sheriff slammed one leg against the back of the knees of his attacker. Zack went down as the lawman landed several hard punches to his face. Matheson's sight was hazy, but he thought Johnstone was unconscious.

The sheriff struggled to his feet as gunshots sounded. Through his slowly clearing vision, Boyd saw two men run from the shack.

"Stop right now!" Adams called out the warning as he stepped from behind the dilapidated structure. For the sake of his own skin, Clay should have forgotten the warning and started shooting first, Matheson thought. A sense of pride coursed through the sheriff. His deputy was not the kind of man who shirked duty and took the easy way.

A barrage of gunshots resulted in one of the robbers dropping to the ground. The other headed for a grove of trees, where horses' neighs could be heard.

Matheson quickly moved toward his own horse, which was tethered nearby. As he mounted the roan, a horse broke from the grove of trees in a gallop.

His vision now completely cleared, Matheson rode swiftly to his deputy. Adams was rising from a crouch after examining the man he had shot.

"Tie up Johnstone, then follow me." He pointed toward the fleeing Russ Cavanaugh. "That guy must have the money."

"I can't believe that Zack—" Clay's face was pale. He had just killed a man.

Matheson caressed his jaw. "I can." He took off after the thief.

Russ Cavanaugh spurred his horse mercilessly. The steed had rested some but had been ridden hard for most of the day. Cavanaugh had left the bay saddled in case a quick getaway was required. For a moment the outlaw thought wistfully about the two fresh horses standing unsaddled in front of the line shack.

He turned his head and saw the lawman approaching from behind at a fast, steady pace. Firing on any target while riding a horse was a very impractical move, but Russ Cavanaugh had never been a practical man. He frantically grabbed his pistol and sent two shots in the lawdog's direction. His pursuer didn't even duck.

Cavanaugh holstered his gun as a tear cut across his cheek. He had failed again. The judge would not forgive him. The judge never forgave. Russ knew that he would somehow be humiliated in front of the rest of the gang.

That is, if he made it back to the hideout. A shot was fired behind him; a warning shot. He was being ordered to surrender.

Russ Cavanaugh doesn't surrender, he thought to himself as he raked the sides of the bay. The action did little good. The horse was unable to run any faster. The lawman was now almost beside him.

This time, Cavanaugh figured he couldn't miss. As he

went for his gun, he felt a collision with a powerful force. The lawdog had jumped him! Cavanaugh plunged from the horse, but one foot remained caught in a stirrup. The outlaw was viciously dragged along the ground as if the bay was seeking revenge for the abuse he had suffered.

Boyd Matheson hit the dirt, rolled, and sprang to his feet. He watched the outlaw being dragged by his horse, then suddenly break free. The horse didn't stop but slowed to a lope.

Matheson drew his gun; then his entire body seemed to lurch into a harsh cough. The sheriff had to bend over and, for a moment, feared that he might fall. As the hacking subsided, the lawman straightened and saw his prey squirming like a snake through the low grass. Matheson remembered seeing a pistol fly from the bank robber's hand when the two men did a fast drop to the ground.

The sheriff wanted to run toward the outlaw, but the tightness in his chest told him that was not an option. Colt .45 in hand, the lawman moved at a brisk pace toward the bank robber.

"Don't move!" Matheson began to cough again and fired a warning shot to cover it.

As he drew near the crook, the sheriff could see that the man was still a comfortable distance from his gun. One foot was missing a boot. "On your feet, mister." Matheson spoke in a clipped manner. His chest threatened another eruption.

"Don't think I can stand."

"Try." Matheson darted his eyes sideways to see Clay Adams approaching on horseback. The sheriff pointed toward the outlaw's bay, which was now grazing with

Matheson's roan at a fair distance away but still within eye range.

"Get the horses." Matheson coughed as he spoke. "The money is probably in the bay's saddlebags."

"Sure." Adams paused, then asked, "You okay?"

"Get the horses." Matheson inhaled and swallowed hard to stifle another cough.

Chapter Three

"There's no jail anywheres that can hold me, Sheriff." Russ Cavanaugh snarled theatrically from behind bars.

Matheson smirked and shook his head. "Yeah, you're a real hard case, Cavanaugh."

The sheriff and his companion then looked at the man who sat hunched over in the cell next to Cavanaugh. "Zack, this man is Beau Kibler." The sheriff nodded toward the intense, scholarly-looking man who stood beside him. "He puts out the newspaper. If you'd like, you can tell him your side of the story. Might help some."

Zack Johnstone had his face buried in his hands. He didn't respond.

The sheriff and the newspaperman left the jail area and returned to the office. "This may sound strange,

24

Boyd." Kibler looked a bit sheepish. "But I feel sorry for Johnstone."

Beau Kibler was a handsome man with a broad face framed by a mass of red hair. Beau rarely thought about going to a barber.

"I'm sure this is the first time Zack has been mixed up in something like this," Matheson replied. "Clay has gone to the Lazy J to tell Ezra what happened. Ezra's just starting to get over the loss of his wife, and now—" The sheriff suddenly switched topics. "Beau, I appreciate your putting out a—what is it called?"

"An extra. Extra edition."

"Yeah, folks need to know fast that the money is back in the bank. Word of mouth isn't good enough. A lot of men do their jawing in a saloon, where tall tales can step on the truth pretty quick. That's why I'm glad you've come to town, Beau. We need a good newspaper."

Kibler's obvious surprise at the compliment indicated that he didn't receive many. "Thanks, Sheriff. I, uh, thank you."

Clay Adams stepped into the sheriff's office accompanied by Ezra Johnstone. Both men were silent and grim.

Boyd Matheson stood up from his desk. "Ezra, I'm sorry."

Ezra Johnstone nodded his head. "May I see my boy?"

The three men walked back into the jail area. Zack stood up and looked his father in the eye. "It's true. What they say about me, Father, it's true."

Ezra was overwhelmed by the sight of his son in a

jail cell. His face mirrored the mass of emotions that battled inside him. "Why?"

Nobody answered.

Beau Kibler finished drying his hands, then spoke to his one employee. "We're finished for tonight, Tobias. The good citizens of Gradyville have been assured that their money is safe."

"Folks appreciate some good news now and again." Tobias was a young man, barely in his twenties, with arms made strong by five years of laboring in the mines. He considered operating a printing press to be clean, pleasant work.

"Tomorrow we'll set the type on the next installment of the Dickens novel."

"That will sure make my wife happy!"

"Confess, Tobias, you enjoy reading that Englishman as much as Molly does." The two men laughed and exchanged good-nights as Tobias departed.

Alone in the office, Beau Kibler felt tired and yet restless. He picked up a copy of the extra. "The *Gradyville Gazette*," he said to himself, returning the paper to a small table. "Wonder what my former colleagues at the *Philadelphia Gazette* would think about that."

Beau had fallen in love with the West and left Philadelphia to start a paper of his own in the Arizona Territory. At least, that was the story he told everyone. People didn't need to know about the beautiful rich girl who had abruptly broken off a romance with a struggling newspaper reporter at her father's orders.

Beau was deep in his private thoughts as he left the

office and began to walk toward the small house where he lived on the north side of town.

"You the newspaper fella?"

Kibler didn't know if the man now walking beside him on the boardwalk had approached from the opposite direction or caught up with him from behind. The man's flat-brimmed hat was pulled down low, and in the darkness Beau couldn't get a good look at his face.

"Ah, yes . . . yes, I am." The journalist shook the past from his mind and looked around. He and his companion seemed to have the town to themselves.

"I know something that should be in that paper of yours."

Beau didn't recognize the voice. "Oh?"

"Could we step aside for a minute?"

"Sure."

Beau followed his companion into an alley. Surrounded by darkness, he cursed himself for being so stupid, but his insight came too late.

The newspaper man awoke to pain and a complete lack of light. The throbbing in his head was from being knocked unconscious. The tight blindfold and the gag in his mouth didn't make matters any better.

Kibler fought to contain the panic that flared inside him. After all, he was still alive. His captors could have easily killed him if that had been their intent. He knew there had to be more than one person involved, because he had been facing the man who approached him on the boardwalk when a pain exploded in the back of his skull.

His hands and feet were bound, and his entire body

was being assaulted by a series of hard bumps. The newsman figured that he was under a pile of blankets in the back of a swiftly moving buckboard. That would have been an easy way to transport him out of Gradyville without anyone noticing.

The buckboard halted. Beau was lifted up and flung across a horse. The reporter had lost all sense of time and direction. He could hear the sound of an occasional coyote but realized that would provide little help if he tried to retrace where his captors were taking him.

When the horse finally stopped, Kibler was yanked off the steed and thrown to the ground. The ropes around his feet were cut, and he was jerked back upward. He could barely stand.

"This way." Beau was shoved from behind and lost his balance as his ankles collided with something hard. The reporter fell onto some wooden planks, and he noted the hollowness of the thud. He seemed to be on a porch.

Kibler was roughly lifted back onto his feet. He could hear a door open, and the footsteps took on a more solid sound. He was pushed into a chair: his hands were cut free, the blindfold removed, and the gag taken from his mouth. Beau could see two men standing on either side of him, but he was too limp to pay them much heed.

"Wait here," one of the outlaws said. "When the judge comes in, you stand up. And don't say nothin' till the judge talks, understand?"

"Yes." The two owlhoots hastily departed. They had been gone for a few minutes before Beau realized that he hadn't even looked at their faces. At that moment, he didn't care.

The door opened again, and a tall man dressed elegantly in a black suit with a string tie walked in. Beau stood up and quickly noted that he was in a large room with one window beside the front door, and a small table was a couple of feet in front of him. A lantern on the table shot a flickering yellow glow across the room.

The man in the expensive suit walked slowly around the table and sat down. Beau noted that the chair behind the table was much bigger than the one he had been plopped into.

After settling into the chair, the newcomer ignored Beau and concentrated on some papers that were lying on the table. He glanced up from the paperwork and pretended to notice Kibler for the first time. "You may be seated."

As Beau sat down, his well-dressed companion continued to speak. "You are Mr. Beau Kibler, correct?"

"Yes."

"Your Honor!" The reply was fast and harsh.

"Pardon?" Beau said.

"Your Honor," the man behind the desk repeated. "You will address me as Your Honor or Judge."

"Yes—Your Honor."

"My full name is Lewis Rutherford Cavanaugh." The judge leaned back and seemed to relax a bit. "You are the owner of the *Gradyville Gazette*?"

"Yes, Your Honor."

"And what does the owner of a newspaper do?"

Cavanaugh's voice had taken on a friendly demeanor. Beau tried to maintain the cordiality. "The owner of a small-town paper in the West has to do just about everything. I sell advertising, write the editorials, report on what is going on in town; I even help to set the type. Right now I can only afford to have one man helping me. I used to work for a paper in Philadelphia. I was a full-time reporter there."

The judge gave a whimsical laugh. "Be patient, Mr. Kibler. Civilization is coming to the West."

Judge Cavanaugh certainly looked civilized. He was a tall man with black hair, an angular face, and what people back East would call classical features. His prominent cheekbones, chin, and nose were perfectly proportioned, as if chiseled by a sculptor. His pencil-thin mustache added to the distinguished appearance.

"Tell me, Mr. Kibler, do you plan to start printing the truth about me in the *Gradyville Gazette*?"

"I don't understand—Your Honor."

"You need to inform the folks of Gradyville that the Arizona Territory is blessed with a modern-day Robin Hood. Judge Lewis Rutherford Cavanaugh is a man who takes from the rich and gives to the poor."

A sense of rage came over Beau Kibler. He was angry with himself for even briefly trying to humor the killer who sat in front of him. "I already have printed the truth about you." Beau's voice suddenly boomed with sarcasm. "Your Honor!"

"And what truth is that, Mr. Kibler?"

Beau could hear a stirring from outside. The judge's henchmen were not far away. Kibler lowered his voice, but the anger was still there. "When you were on the bench, you took bribes and set some of the worst criminals in the Arizona Territory free. Then you resigned and began to head a gang consisting largely of the snakes you turned loose. This gang is the most vicious in the West. Your hands are stained with blood—Your Honor."

To Beau's astonishment, the judge began to laugh. "Mr. Kibler, your prose is becoming quite purple. You can do better than that."

That response only intensified the reporter's anger. His voice almost became a hiss. "I've read those newspaper stories, even a few dime novels, about your being a Robin Hood. How much money did you pay those writers?"

Cavanaugh continued to laugh. "Less than you would think. Guess why."

Now it was Kibler's turn to laugh. "Some men will do anything for a quick, dirty dollar."

"Because money and power are all that matters. I didn't have to pay those writers too much because they had the good sense to believe me when I told them that one day I will be the governor of this territory and be in a position to enrich them for life."

"Governor!"

"First I will need to hold a lesser position—mayor of Yuma is what I have in mind."

"You plan to buy the votes?"

"Some. But I will get most of them the same way that politicians have gotten votes for years. I'll tell people what they want to hear. After all, who would vote against Robin Hood?"

"Your Honor, I assure you that the *Gradyville Gazette* will do nothing to aid you in your attempt to turn Arizona into Sherwood Forest."

Cavanaugh smiled in a mildly amused manner, then took a pipe and a pouch of tobacco from his coat. He spoke as he filled the pipe. "That is a decision you will come to regret. But there is another task I have for you, and you will not have to lie."

"And what's that, Judge?"

Cavanaugh patted the tobacco firmly into the pipe. "Do you study history, Mr. Kibler?"

"Yes, as much as I can."

"Have you noticed that throughout history powerful men have shared a similar problem?"

Beau was tempted to say that men who gain power often abuse it, but he settled for, "I don't follow you."

The judge put the pipe into his mouth and set a match to it. After a few puffs, he turned to his prisoner. "The curse of the powerful man is that he always has a weakling for a son. It started at the very beginning of time. Isaac was a strong patriarch, but his son, Jacob, had a backbone of straw. Nothing much has changed since then."

Angry puffs of smoke fired from the pipe. Cavanaugh's eyes pierced through the haze as he continued to talk to the reporter. "I value my horses and mules more than I do my son, Russ. He killed his mother when he came into this world and has been worthless ever since."

"Russ won't be causing you any more trouble, Your Honor. He's in jail in Gradyville, and soon he'll probably pay the ultimate price for killing Rollie Jensen."

"I know all that. But, you see, I can't let Russ hang, pleasant as that notion may be."

A mocking smile suddenly creased Beau's face. "Why, of course not, Your Honor. Robin Hood would never allow his son to dangle at the end of a rope."

Cavanaugh's eyes continued to emit fire. "I would be viewed as a weakling, a man who couldn't protect his own family. A man who was defeated by a lowly tin star." The judge pointed his pipe at Kibler. "Tell the good citizens of Gradyville that they have until Wednesday at noon to release Russ Cavanaugh, or the gang that you called the most vicious in the West will destroy the town!"

"Be warned, Your Honor, that that 'tin star' you were talking about is one of the best, and he has a terrific deputy. Besides all that, Gradyville has citizens who know how to protect themselves."

"Boyd Matheson will crumble very shortly. You see, I have learned over the years how to break people's will, Mr. Kibler. The citizens of Gradyville will be no different." The judge shouted toward the door. "Okay!" He glanced back at Beau. "Enjoy your trip back, and keep in mind that offer I made you. You could be a wealthy man someday."

The two henchmen reentered the cabin. They obviously intended to bind, gag, and blindfold the reporter. Beau jumped from his chair and landed a fast punch to the cheekbone of one of the owlhoots, who staggered backward. Kibler turned toward the second outlaw but was seconds too slow. A pistol slammed against the side of his head. The reporter collapsed to the floor as his vision blurred and a feeling of nausea enveloped him.

"Like I said, Mr. Kibler, civilization is coming to the West, but I fear that it is coming rather slowly."

Laughter was the last thing Kibler heard before he passed out.

Chapter Four

"As you gentlemen can see, I'm ready for tonight's prayer meeting. I've got on my new boots." The pastor looked down at his feet. "I think these things add an inch to my height. Wearing these boots, I stand at five feet. Well, almost."

As the two lawmen laughed, Boyd Matheson noted that the pastor often made jokes about his small physical stature. Frank Steuben, known in Gradyville as Reverend Stubby, was the town's mayor and schoolteacher as well as being pastor of its only church.

"I'd sure love to be at the meeting tonight to hear Laurel sing and play the new piano," Clay Adams said. He was standing with Matheson and Reverend Stubby in the sheriff's office.

"I was looking forward to it myself." The soft look that appeared in Boyd Matheson's eyes triggered an uneasiness in his deputy. That look seemed to appear whenever Laurel's name was mentioned.

The clergyman didn't notice Clay's discomfort; he gave his two companions a genial smile. "I wish both of you could come. Todd Wheeler was kind enough to donate the Silver Creek Saloon's old piano to the church. That musical instrument has played "Whiskey, Wine, and Wild, Wild Women" for the last time."

The lawmen laughed again. "Clay and I may not be there," Matheson said, "but with the piano and all, you should have a good crowd."

"We always get a good crowd for the Wednesday night prayer meeting, thanks to Prayerful Patty."

"Who?" Matheson asked.

"I'm sure both of you gentlemen have heard Patty Larson's long, loud prayers. She prays aloud for all the men she has seen staggering out of the saloons during the week. Of course, she names every one of them. She prays for those women who lost their temper and yelled at their husbands. Once again, we hear all the names. Prayerful Patty is a fount of gossip. If she ever started a newspaper, she'd put Beau Kibler out of business."

"Speaking of Beau, have—"

Reverend Stubby anticipated Matheson's question. "I saw Beau before coming here. He won't be at the meeting tonight. Getting out the Wednesday edition of the paper was hard on him. He needs a night's rest to nurse that concussion."

Matheson nodded. "Beau came to me even before he went to see Doc Evans. We're going to have to guard Russ Cavanaugh constantly. After all, the judge's ultimatum ran out at noon today. We'll need two men on duty at all times. Hank and Orin Mellor have already agreed to help. They can get other family members to lend a hand at the livery."

"Hank used to boast that he could handle a shotgun better than anyone in the Territory." Clay smiled broadly as he spoke. The young lawman felt completely comfortable now that the conversation had shifted away from Laurel. "These days, he says that his son is even better. No one who has seen what Orin can do with a double-barrel would argue the point."

"Yes, and I'll do what I can." Reverend Stubby glanced toward the jail area. "I'll be here talking with Zack Johnstone every day. He's one sorrowful young man. . . ."

As the mayor continued to speak, Boyd mused on how odd it might seem to an outsider to hear this man who didn't quite stand at five feet, even in his new boots, and who wore the black frock coat of a pastor, to be volunteering to help guard a prisoner. But no one who knew Reverend Stubby would be surprised. The pastor could handle a gun better than most in the town.

When the sheriff's attention returned to the conversation, Clay Adams was speaking. "From what I can tell, most folks aren't too worried about Judge Cavanaugh's ultimatum. Guess that's not too surprising; hard cases are always making crazy threats."

"Yes, but I'm afraid it goes further than that." A look of sadness creased the pastor's face. "Some people in this town actually think of Judge Cavanaugh as a hero." Stubby shook his head as if vanquishing the melancholy. "Now, if you gentlemen will excuse me, I need to get to the church. I don't want to be late. Prayerful Patty may start praying about me."

As Reverend Stubby approached the Gradyville Community Church, he saw a large number of people milling about outside, chatting with one another and enjoying the cool evening. The pastor noticed a group of boys huddled around nine-year-old Curt Brock, who was wearing something on his left hand that piqued Stubby's curiosity.

As he approached the kids, he could hear Curt's enthusiastic voice. "The ball is hard and can really hurt. You can't play without a glove."

"Curt, is that a baseball glove you're wearing?" Reverend Stubby's voice was almost as enthusiastic as the boy's.

"Yes, Preacher!" Curt proudly held up his left hand.

"Baseball is the thing Curt misses most about St. Louis." Silas Brock, Curt's father, was standing a few feet away with his wife and daughter. "We ordered a baseball and bat for him from a catalogue. It arrived just in time for his birthday." He nodded toward his wife. "Aimee made the glove for him."

Stubby looked at the circle of boys. "You know, fellas, just maybe I can get some of the ladies in the church to make us up a bunch of baseball gloves. Then, some Saturday afternoon, we can get together here in front of the church, and Mr. Brock and I can teach all of you how to play baseball."

There was a loud chorus of cheers, but one skeptic shouted out, "Preacher, do you know how to play baseball?"

"I sure do!" Stubby replied. "I played baseball while I was in Boston. That's where I learned how to be a pastor." He looked at Curt. "I bet you can guess what position I play."

"Well . . ." The boy looked embarrassed.

"Come on," the pastor encouraged him, "don't be shy."

The boy spoke hesitantly. "Shortstop?"

"You're right! How did you guess?"

The boys exploded with laughter. Stubby walked over to Jane, Curt's seven-year-old sister, who was standing beside her mother. He talked with the child for a few minutes, realizing that she might be feeling a bit ignored with all of the attention being focused on her brother. Then he turned to Jane's father. "Hope you didn't mind my volunteering you for an afternoon of baseball."

"Not at all, Reverend."

"Aimee, could you come up with some activity for the girls? I don't want them to feel left out."

"Of course, Reverend Steuben. I'd be happy to."

The pastor exchanged a few more words with the couple, then turned back toward the church, where piano music could be heard from within. The clergyman stepped onto the church's small porch, glanced through the opened front door, and saw Laurel Remick rehearsing on the piano while several people watched. Many of the watchers were young men, which didn't surprise the Reverend. Laurel Remick was a strikingly beautiful young woman, made even more so by the church's kerosene lamps, which seemed to create a soft glow that danced around her blond hair.

"Maybe Clay Adams should be guarding his fiancée instead of some killer," Reverend Stubby whispered mischievously to himself.

Stubby turned his attention to the folks outside. Ezra Johnstone was not among them. The pastor made a mental note to visit Ezra the next day. Ezra Johnstone was going through a very deep valley and needed to be reassured that he was always welcome at church.

The sound of hoofbeats caused the pastor to look east. Maybe Ezra was coming after all and bringing Jimmy, his sixteen-year-old boy, and Esther, his only daughter, who was fourteen.

No, there were six riders, and all of them appeared to be men, heading directly for the church. Stubby squinted against the red sky and looked carefully at the approaching horsemen. Why were they riding so fast? And there was something strange about their appearance. As the riders drew closer, the pastor's curiosity turned to alarm. The riders were all wearing bandannas over their faces.

"Inside the church, everyone!"

"The meeting don't start for another five minutes, Reverend," came a voice from the crowd.

"Inside—now!"

The second shout was followed by a barrage of gunshots. Stubby saw at least two people go down but couldn't help them. Bullets continued to fly, and the crowd now stampeded into the church. The pastor waited until everyone who could make it was inside the building, then slammed the door.

"Get down!" This time no one needed prodding to

follow the pastor's direction. People scrambled behind the pews and hit the floor.

A shout came from outside. "You jaspers got warned! But you didn't turn Russ Cavanaugh loose. Now you'll all die!"

"You yellow snakes!" Reverend Stubby yelled back. "You knew no one would carry a gun to a church meeting. You're cowards, all of you!"

Derisive laughter sounded from outside. Stubby crouched in a jackknife position. He looked out the side windows, saw no one there, then ran toward the front of the church and the small room that was a few feet beside the pulpit. As he entered the room, he could see Laurel Remick, who had been crouched near the piano, following him.

"Reverend Steuben." Her voice was almost a whisper. "What are—"

"Praise God for a congregation that believes in keeping its pastor poor." Stubby also spoke in a whisper as he grabbed a Winchester that was propped in a corner. "If I owned a house instead of living here, my guns would be far away right now." He grabbed a .44 pistol from a holster that was lying on the desk and glanced out the door of what was both the pastor's study and his living quarters.

"Perfect!" he said to the young woman. "Orin Mellor is behind the pew closest to the doors. You stay here. Get down low."

Winchester in one hand and the .44 in the other, Stubby ran down the center aisle of the church, not slowing as he handed Orin the pistol. The clergyman stopped at the church's only doors and listened carefully. He could hear the neighing of a horse and the sound of liquid being splashed on the left side of the building. He turned toward Orin, who was now standing beside him. The two men exchanged a silent communication, then Stubby flung open one of the doors and stepped hastily onto the porch.

Stubby saw a masked horseman lighting a match. The outlaw had barely turned toward the pastor when the Winchester fired, and both horseman and match plunged to the ground. The match was a safe distance from the kerosene splashed onto a corner of the church.

Stubby hit the boards as bullets whizzed over him. Orin stepped onto the porch. His first shot hit the nearest outlaw, who bent over on his horse while holding on to his gun. Hoofbeats could be heard coming from the center of town.

Orin fired at another outlaw who was farther away from the church, while Stubby fired in the general direction of the four remaining owlhoots. Both men missed but not by much. Two more shots came from the direction of the approaching hoofbeats. The remaining outlaws were dazed and uncertain. They quickly rode off, ignoring the wail of their injured comrade.

Boyd Matheson holstered his pistol as he rode up to the church. "Not much chance of catching up with them. The sun is almost gone. Is Laurel okay?"

"She's fine," Stubby quickly replied.

"Good. Uh . . ." Matheson stammered for a moment, then continued to speak as he dismounted. "That'll be the first thing Clay asks me—"

The injured gunman slipped off his horse and began twitching in pain on the ground. Matheson crouched over the fallen outlaw, who still had an inch or so of life in him. The gunman's holster was empty. Matheson did a fast walk to the corner of the church where another body lay beside an empty canteen that reeked of kerosene. Only a quick glance was required to know that the second outlaw was dead.

Matheson turned his head as he heard cries and shouts from behind him. A group of people was forming in a wide circle.

Boyd stepped into the crowd and looked at the horrible sight. "Silas and Aimee Brock. They were good people, never harmed anyone." Matheson's shock quickly turned to anger as he saw the two other bodies. "Jane and Curt—they're only little children. . . ."

Reverend Stubby crouched over the body of the nine-year-old boy. The baseball glove, still on his left hand, was soaked with blood. "The other three are gone, but Curt is still alive. Barely. We need to get him to Doc Evans quick."

They did get him to the doctor quickly. But it wasn't quick enough. The boy died an hour later.

Chapter Five

Reverend Stubby looked at the grim-faced assembly of people now gathered in the church and reflected on what a change twenty-four hours had brought to the town. Only the previous evening people were gathering together to sing and listen to the new piano. That afternoon the town had buried four of its citizens, two of them children. Through the church's open doors, the pastor could see Hank Mellor standing guard. Evil seemed to be everywhere, the pastor thought.

Stubby was sitting with Boyd Matheson on the platform in front of the church's choir loft. The pastor checked his watch, then stood up and led the group in a brief prayer. As he opened his eyes, the clergyman saw that some women were crying. He wanted to say something comforting but decided against it. On this night he was performing in his capacity as the town's mayor.

"All of you know what happened here last night," the mayor said. "I have called a town meeting for us to discuss how we are going to meet this threat to Gradyville. I'll now turn the meeting over to Sheriff Matheson."

Matheson stood up and looked over the crowd carefully, as if trying to briefly make eye contact with everyone there. "I owe this town an apology. When I first heard that Judge Cavanaugh gave us an ultimatum about releasing his son, I just took it for granted that when we didn't meet his deadline, the judge would attack the sheriff's office to set Russ Cavanaugh free. I didn't know he would kill innocent folks. When we heard the shots last night, I came to see what was going on and left Clay Adams to guard the prisoner. At first I thought the shots were just a trick to get us away from the sheriff's office."

"It's not your fault, Boyd." Doc Evans spoke from the front pew. "No one could have known."

"I am certain of this much," the sheriff said. "Those gunmen killed the entire Brock family because they happened to be in easy firing range. No other reason. They wanted to kill everyone at the meeting last night and thought they could because folks don't carry guns to church. We are dealing with a new kind of enemy and will be for a while. The circuit judge won't be in Gradyville for another three weeks."

"And exactly how will we be dealing with this enemy, Sheriff?"

The question was shouted from a back pew by Naomi Willis. Matheson was surprised by the edge in her voice but didn't show it. "That's a good question, Naomi, and an important one."

The sheriff paused to collect his thoughts, then continued. "Until Russ Cavanaugh is tried and, if found guilty, hanged, this town needs to be ready for an attack at any time. I want those men who are able, to carry guns at all times and be prepared to use them. That includes church meetings. Reverend Stubby has talked with the fathers of his schoolchildren. There will be someone on guard outside the schoolhouse when the young ones are receiving their lessons. We need to think differently, to always be prepared for an attack."

Ezra Johnstone held up a hand. Matheson nodded in his direction, and the rancher stood up to speak. "Sheriff, I need to know what you're going to do to protect my boy. There's a good chance that, sooner or later, there will be gunplay at the sheriff's office. My boy is in the cell right next to Russ Cavanaugh. You must release him tonight! I'll give you my word that Zack will be here when the circuit judge arrives. He'll stand trial and take his punishment. But it's not right for him to be locked up where he'll likely be in the path of a stray bullet."

Ezra's body was shaking as he sat down.

Matheson spoke slowly and in a calm manner. "We can't release Zack, Ezra."

"Why not?" the rancher shouted back.

"Because we'd have to do the same thing for anyone we might arrest over the next three weeks. I can't let every owlhoot in this town stay free because Russ Cavanaugh is in jail."

Ezra said nothing, but Matheson was chilled by the strong emotions that played across the rancher's face.

The lawman hoped that Ezra could keep those emotions under control.

"Russ Cavanaugh is the one you should release!" Naomi Willis rose to her feet. "Killing only leads to more killing! We want Gradyville to be a decent place, not some wide-open town like Tombstone. Let Judge Cavanaugh have his no-good son, and let this town live in peace."

A murmur of agreement spread through the crowd. A few people patted Naomi on the shoulder as she sat down.

Walter Jarrett jumped to his feet. "She's right! The railroad is coming to our town. Gradyville is becoming prosperous. A lot of us have worked hard to make it that way. We don't want this place destroyed because of one outlaw. Besides, Miss Willis made a valuable point. It's high time this town acted civilized. Prisoners need to be rehabilitated, not hanged. Turn Russ Cavanaugh loose!"

Jarrett's words were met with several shouts of approval. Reverend Stubby rose from his chair, his voice soaring over the commotion. "This town must never surrender to evil! If we can be cowed by threats from lawless, venal men, then we will be the puppets of lawless, venal men. There will always be evil among us, and that evil must be confronted. Otherwise, there will be more people like the Brock family, innocents who are gunned down at the whim of the wicked. Civilization is a fragile thing that must always be cherished and protected, or it will be lost."

The pastor's remarks were followed by silence,

broken only by an "Amen, Preacher!" shouted by Cassius Remick, the owner of Remick's General Store.

"Thanks, Cassius, but I'm acting as the mayor tonight."

"It may not be Sunday morning"—Laurel, Cassius' granddaughter, spoke with gratitude—"but we needed the sermon. Thank you, Reverend Steuben."

The young woman's remarks were followed by similar statements that issued forth from various people in the church. The mayor gave a silent sigh of relief, then spoke aloud. "I understand the sentiments that were expressed earlier in this meeting. I hold Naomi and Walter in the highest of regard, and I assure all of you that guns will be employed only when they are needed." Stubby turned to the sheriff. "Boyd, I turn it back to you."

Matheson looked across the gathering. "Anybody else want to say anything? Any questions?"

"Yes, Sheriff." Beau Kibler remained seated as he spoke. Matheson noticed that Kibler continued to write in a small notebook that he had on his knee. The reporter seemed always to have one of those notebooks with him, and, more often than not, it was opened.

"We know that two outlaws were shot during the attack on the church last night," Kibler said. "The man who was shot by the reverend died instantly. But the other man, the one Orin Mellor hit, is still alive, and—"

Matheson frowned. "That outlaw died in Doc Evans' office about two hours ago. It's too bad. I would have liked to have a talk with him."

There were a few other questions, most of them from folks who wanted assurance that they were safe and that matters would soon return to normal. Matheson had to firmly restate that constant vigilance was now needed and would be for some time.

After the meeting was over, Matheson, Clay Adams, and Reverend Stubby gathered in the sheriff's office to exchange ideas and take some comfort in one another's company.

"What's eating at you, Boyd?" the deputy asked as Matheson paced about the office with a cup of coffee in hand.

"Walter Jarrett," Matheson answered. "He was sure acting out of character tonight. The owner of the Roman Holiday Saloon was backing up Naomi Willis— the president of the local temperance union. Jarrett can't stand the sight of Naomi."

"And all that talk about rehabilitation." Clay poured himself a cup of coffee from the pot on the small stove. He glanced at Stubby, who declined with a slight shake of his head, then continued. "Where did Jarrett get such fancy notions?"

The pastor laughed out loud. "Until tonight, Walter's idea of rehabilitation was to read a prisoner the Twenty-third Psalm before you hanged him."

Matheson stopped his pacing and took a sip of java. "I don't think Jarrett knew what *rehabilitation* meant— until recently."

"What do you mean?" the clergyman asked.

"I'm not quite sure, myself. But I do know this. Jarrett leaves town a lot, usually late at night. Clay and I often see him riding off. He can be gone days at a time. I asked him about it once. He says he has to attend to business."

Stubby made a quizzical face. "Why would a saloon owner always be needing to leave town? Todd Wheeler never goes on business trips, and the Silver Creek is a much larger and more successful operation than the Roman Holiday."

As he listened, Clay Adams admitted to himself that he had not paid enough attention to Jarrett's odd behavior. He considered himself fortunate to be working with a man he could learn from, a man he admired and respected like Boyd Matheson. For a moment, almost against his own will, he thought about the special glances that occasionally shot between Boyd and Laurel, and he wondered, for probably the thousandth time, if he should ask his fiancée what it all meant.

Matheson's voice brought the deputy back to the matter of Walter Jarrett. "Reverend, can you help Clay tonight?"

"Sure."

"After the meeting, I heard Jarrett tell one of his bartenders that he wouldn't be in at the Roman Holiday tomorrow morning—might not be back til evening. Think maybe I'll find out where he's going to be."

Chapter Six

The town hall meeting had been a boon to the saloon business. After the meeting was over, a large number of men headed for the Silver Creek or Roman Holiday saloons to rehash what had been discussed at the church and to assert, many times over, their opinions as to what needed to be done about the threats from Judge Cavanaugh.

Walter Jarrett did not leave his establishment until business had diminished to a couple of all-night poker games. As he untied his bay from the hitch rail in front of the Roman Holiday, he glanced at the sheriff on the opposite boardwalk, then mounted seemingly without a second thought.

The lawman waited for about three minutes after his prey was out of sight, then mounted his own horse. As he trailed Jarrett from a comfortable distance, Matheson felt a bit foolish. After all, the saloon owner was doing nothing too suspicious. He often left town late at night, sometimes exchanging nods with Matheson, who would be on a round.

There was no law against riding a horse late at night, but Reverend Stubby had a point. Why would a saloon owner need to make so many business trips? And then there was the matter of Jarrett's backing up a woman he hated at the town hall meeting and all his talk about "rehabilitation," the kind of fancy word Jarrett never used.

But from what Matheson knew of him, Judge Cavanaugh was the kind of man who prided himself on fancy words.

The sheriff laughed quietly to himself, then whispered to his horse. "I may have you on a wild goose chase tonight. When a man gets desperate, he sometimes grabs at any fool notion that comes along."

Matheson halted the horse and pulled his field glasses from a saddlebag. The moon was considerably less than full, but it still shone brightly. Walter Jarrett was making good time, his horse moving in a brisk, easy manner. The steed had made this run many times before.

The sheriff kept his roan at a slower pace on the flat, narrow trail. It was pleasant being out of town, where the sounds of drunken fools shouting in bars didn't interrupt the quiet of a cool Arizona night. Matheson wondered how many more of these nights he had left to enjoy.

For a moment, his mind shifted back to a small Texas town and his first job as a lawman. He had met his wife,

Ann, there, and they had one year of happiness together before . . .

The image came back to him as it still did occasionally. A sixteen-year-old cowboy riding into town for good times, firing his gun into the air to let everyone know of his arrival—the type of foolish thing cowboys did all the time. But the kid didn't really have control of his horse and didn't realize how low he was firing. One of those bullets slammed into Ann's head, killing her instantly and killing the child forming inside her.

Matheson had turned in his star soon after that and become a drifter—at least, that was how he thought of himself. Most people called him a gunfighter. For close to ten years Boyd Matheson wandered throughout the West, accepting jobs from folks who needed the skills he had to offer. But he never violated the law he had once enforced. The men Matheson had dispatched to boot hill needed to go there.

Everything had changed when Boyd Matheson rode into Gradyville, Arizona, a town ruled at the time by a despot. The citizens had implored him to become their sheriff and bring justice to the town. For reasons he didn't completely understand, he'd agreed to do it.

A smile cut across the lawman's face as he continued to keep an eye on his distant prey. He had to be honest with himself: Laurel Remick was one reason he had agreed to become sheriff. She was the first woman to interest him since the death of Ann. But then the doc had given him some unwelcome news, and he realized that he needed to keep a distance from the young woman.

He was happy that Laurel was now engaged to Clay Adams. Clay was a fine man. Matheson's plan was . . .

The sheriff quickly guided his horse off the trail and behind two scraggly mesquite trees that stood together. They were entering a hilly region, and Walter Jarrett was riding up the largest of those hills. From his lower angle, Matheson watched the saloon owner through his field glasses. Jarrett's horse maintained a steady, fast stride. The bay was still riding over familiar ground.

Matheson waited until Jarrett was out of sight, then hastily returned the field glasses to one of his saddlebags. Following the bar owner up the hill was a surprisingly easy task. Instead of the narrow trail he had been expecting, Boyd found a wide, well-traveled road. Still, the lawman was cautious. He would make an easy target, and the surrounding rocks could hide a lookout.

As he came over the top of the hill, the lawman saw into a valley shaped like a horseshoe. Jarrett was tying his horse in front of a cabin. Matheson waited until Jarrett was inside, then rode up an ascent to a row of boulders large enough to hide his horse. He dismounted, tethered the animal, then hid behind one of the large rocks and viewed the flatland below with his field glasses.

There were two long clapboard cabins. Boyd figured that the first cabin provided a living quarters. The second cabin, which neighbored it on the right, was much bigger and appeared to be where men did work of some kind. Both structures appeared to have been hastily built. A stable stood far behind.

Walter Jarrett remained inside the first cabin. Matheson quickly moved his gaze about, trying to spot a look-out, but, like the trail that led to it, the area appeared unguarded. If Walter Jarrett was doing anything illegal, he had little concern about the law.

Boyd laughed softly. Maybe he should take that as an insult, he thought. The lawman pulled a Henry rifle from the scabbard of his saddle, then advanced down the slope, carefully looking about without knowing what he was looking for.

His first destination was the stable, from which came the sounds of calmly neighing horses. The stable contained two wagons, both finely built and capable of moving heavy cargo. Pretty much the same thing could be said for the eight horses stabled there.

Good horses and good wagons didn't come cheaply. Walter Jarrett had found a way to riches. Matheson left the stable and headed for the building where he figured the work was done. He hoped to discover the nature of the business that had made Jarrett wealthy and had also made him very secretive.

At the back of the building, he peered into a small window that paralleled a similar window in the front. Boyd could only see the outlines of apparatuses that, in the darkness, looked strange and sinister. The lawman clucked his tongue as he spotted an unlit kerosene lantern on a table in front of the back window.

The building had both a front and back door. Boyd moved cautiously to the far left side of the building and the back door, which he opened slowly. It didn't creak. The sheriff stepped inside, closed the door, and paused for a moment as his eyes adjusted to the darkness. But he didn't pause long enough. His knee hit something as he moved toward the lantern. He stopped immediately and listened. Whatever he collided with hadn't made much noise. There didn't seem to be any stirring coming from outside. The sheriff continued to creep toward his destination.

Matheson carefully set his Henry against the table that held the kerosene lantern, then patted the area around the lantern until he found the box of matches that he had figured would be there. He bent over and struck a match. Moving in a jackknife position to blanket the flame, Matheson began to inspect the rows of crates that were stacked along thick wooden shelves that lined one wall of the cabin. Each box contained liquor bottles with labels of well-known breweries across the front.

Boyd recalled an article he had read in an eastern newspaper a while back. Several crooks had been arrested in New York City for making their own rotgut and selling it in bottles with phony labels that identified the stuff as coming from legitimate liquor companies.

Walter Jarrett, or someone he knew, must have read that same article. No making tanglefoot and selling it in jugs like a handful of pathetic lowlifes in town did in order to scrounge a few dollars. Walter Jarrett had put his rotgut into bottles with fancy labels and, as a result of his enterprise, become a wealthy man.

Then the lawman wondered if Jarrett was the top dog in this operation. "Could be wrong, but this is a pretty fancy operation for Walter," Matheson whispered to himself.

The flame on the match was moving quickly down the stick. The sheriff extinguished it with a fast shake, pulled the matches from his pocket, and lit another. He then stepped cautiously from the shelf to the odd contraptions that filled much of the long room. A sense of excitement built inside him as he moved the flame over the machinery that comprised an elaborate still and saw exactly how Jarrett produced his counterfeit booze.

The sheriff's excitement turned to something different as he heard footsteps coming from the direction of the other cabin. Instinctively he blew out the match, then grabbed his Henry rifle and crouched low. But the footsteps trudged by the building that housed the still and continued on toward the stable.

Remaining in a crouch, Boyd waddled to the back door and opened it a bit. He wanted to hear the conversation coming from the stable. The lawman didn't have to work his ears too hard. Walter Jarrett's loud voice was booming out as usual. "Tell me, Lenny, on your next trip to Tombstone, do you plan to talk with Beau Cummings about the money he owes us?"

The voice that replied was high pitched and nervous. "Why, yes, sir, I plan to do just that. I'm sure Mr. Cummings will have the money. His business just got a little behind, that's all. He had to delay a payment, but I figured that was okay, what with him being a regular customer and all."

"You figured that was okay, huh?"

Lenny caught the menace in Jarrett's voice. His reply was even more jittery. "Yes, sir, yes, sir, uh, that's how I figured it."

Matheson rose to his feet, still using the door as a shield, and looked around it. There were six men, including Jarrett, standing in front of the stable. A kerosene lantern hanging over the stable door bathed all of them in yellow. Walter Jarrett and four of his henchmen had formed a circle around Lenny. Lenny was easily the youngest of the bunch, still a far distance from twenty.

"Funny thing," Jarrett continued. "I was in Tombstone last week—dropped in on Beau to see what the trouble was. Beau told me there weren't no trouble at all. He paid you on the last run, just like always."

"Guess maybe he forgot—"

"I guess maybe *you* forgot, Lenny. Forgot that you gave Beau Cummings a receipt. I recognized that chicken scratch you call handwriting on the paper—"

"I'm sorry, Mr. Jarrett! Look, I lost a lot of money at cards. Had to pay some hombres back fast. Yeah, I stole the money, but I'll pay it back, honest—"

Jarrett slammed a fist into Lenny's face. The boy dropped to the ground and began to weep. "You fool!" The saloon owner's right hand was still clenched in a fist. "Beau Cummings thinks I'm the real McCoy—a distributor for a booze outfit. You don't do nothing to call attention in a setup like this."

"I'm sorry, Mr. Jarrett. Please, let me talk to the judge, apologize in person."

Walter Jarrett delivered a hard kick to Lenny's ribs. "You don't even mention the judge! When you're here, you're working for me!"

"Yes, sir. I'll do anything I can to help. Please—"

"You're gonna help, all right. I'm using you as an example, in case anyone else gets fool notions about cheating me." Jarrett looked around at the remaining four men. "One of you boys think maybe you could rustle up a rope?"

Harsh laughter filled the night. Jarrett's henchmen were looking forward to a bit of fun—a pleasant diversion from making rotgut and delivering it to saloon owners who didn't have much curiosity about the low prices.

Lenny sprang to his feet and made a desperate attempt to run. Two men grabbed him, hammered his ribs a few times, and then shoved him to the ground. Two other men moved quickly into the stable and came out with a bridled horse. "You'll be plenty comfortable on this fella!" an outlaw shouted as he pointed to the horse. " 'Course, you won't be on him long!"

The wave of laughter couldn't cover Lenny's panicked screams. One of the outlaws shouted something Matheson couldn't understand, then ran toward the front of the cabins. Matheson scuttled inside, closed the door, and crouched down where he couldn't be seen through the front window. For a few minutes there was only the sound of Lenny's cries, accompanied by mocking laughter. Then he could hear the sound of hoofbeats pounding toward the stable.

When Matheson opened the door again, one of the thugs was on a horse, tossing a rope over the branch of a cottonwood that sided the stable. Matheson realized what the owlhoot had been doing during those comparatively quiet moments. A finely-knotted noose hung at the end of the rope.

The horseman tied the other end of the rope to the horn of his saddle. "Ain't never done this before, but, ya know, this here saddle has held cows that weigh more than that scrawny kid!"

Both the laughter and screams increased as Lenny was lifted to his feet. Someone had tied the boy's hands behind his back, probably with a bandanna. Walter Jarrett stood back and lit a cigar as one of his henchmen held the horse that was brought out from the stable, and two others dragged the boy toward it. The owlhoot on the horse waved a knife at the victim. "Don't worry none, kid. Soon as your neck's broke, I'll cut you down nice and easy."

Lenny looked upward and cried out to God for help. Matheson recalled a sermon Reverend Stubby had preached about man serving as God's instrument on earth. "Guess that applies here," he whispered to himself. "I don't see any lightning bolts coming down."

Matheson moved out from behind the door and took two long steps toward the stable. "All of you are under arrest. Hands up. Now!"

"What are you doing here, Matheson?" Walter Jarrett sounded offended, as if the sheriff had barged into his home without knocking.

"I'm stopping a murder, and—"

A bullet whizzed by his ear. Matheson whirled and aimed his Henry toward the well-lit side window of the first cabin. His first shot tore into the chest of a gunman who seemed to explode into oblivion. Matheson dropped to one knee as a barrage of bullets came at him from the stable area. The lawman's second shot hit Walter Jarrett, who collided with the ground as his pistol flew upward and then landed on his belly.

The thug on horseback had seen enough. He cut the rope from his saddle and took off. The other three henchmen evidently thought that a good idea. They fired a few more shots at Matheson, only to keep him distant as they began a run to the front of the cabins and their horses.

Still perched on a knee, the sheriff turned and took another look at the cabin behind him. The light still shone brightly from the window, but there were no shadows to indicate that another gunman might be waiting there.

The sound of frantic hoofbeats filled the air as Matheson cautiously approached Walter Jarrett. Boyd picked the revolver off of Jarrett's stomach and searched him for any other weapons. The saloon owner seemed to be conscious but not comprehending his surroundings. His eyes had a glazed look, and he glanced about restlessly.

Lenny was lying on the ground, crying.

"Stop your blubbering." Matheson spoke in a sharp whisper.

"Yes, sir. Sorry—"

"Did all of the others ride off?"

"Yes. I saw them."

"How about that first cabin? Do you know how many men are in there?"

"Just one, the cook. But you got him good, Sheriff.

That shot went right into his chest, and you can bet there ain't much left of him now. . . ."

Lenny kept talking about the terrific shot Matheson had placed into the cook's chest. The kid was scared and trying to ingratiate himself. The sheriff knew that but still felt angry. Why couldn't the fool cook have just ridden off like the others? He wondered, fleetingly, if most of the men he had killed over the years hadn't been bigger fools than they were outlaws.

"What are you going to do now, Sheriff?"

Lenny's question made the lawman feel strangely edgy. He realized that he had to shake himself out of the mood he was in. "How does your side feel?"

"Hurts bad. Got a couple broken ribs, I think. But I can still get around okay."

"I'll send someone back to bury the cook and take care of other things here. You're going to help me hitch a wagon and get Walter Jarrett into it. I want to keep him alive. He may have some information I can use."

"Yes, sir. Glad to help." Lenny grasped the hand Matheson offered and slowly made it to his feet. He was bent over a bit as he walked with Matheson to the stable.

"How'd you get tied up with an outfit like Jarrett's?" There was a hint of concern in Matheson's voice, but only a hint.

"Just stupid, I guess. Came to Gradyville to find work."

The two men entered the stable and stopped for a moment. Boyd looked around and spotted a side wall where the bridles were hanging. He walked toward them slowly, as he noticed Lenny's pain was increasing. He wanted to keep the boy talking. "My guess is that the first place you stopped at in Gradyville was the Roman Holiday saloon. Jarrett heard you jawing about needing work and offered you a job."

"Yes, sir."

"Did you suspect that Jarrett was pulling something illegal?"

Lenny looked down and nodded. "Jarrett didn't say so right out, but I sorta figured that was the case."

They stopped in front of an impressive array of bridles. Matheson eyed the boy directly. "So, you were working for Jarrett, not the judge?"

A look of discouragement ravaged the young man's face. The judge seemed to represent a pinnacle he had failed to attain. "I was Jarrett's hire. That made me different from the rest."

"What do you mean?"

"This whole operation was the judge's idea. He was the boss man!" A look of awe flared in Lenny's eyes. "Walter Jarrett was only the ramrod. The other fellas were all hired by the judge. I was just brought on because they needed an extra hand. The other fellas are all riding back to the judge's hideout right now."

"Do you know where that is?"

"No, sir. They never tol' me. I know it's somewhere in the hills surrounded by rock and hard ground. Not much chance you can trail those guys."

Matheson turned and displayed more interest in the bridles than he actually had, leaving a moment of silence, which Lenny broke. "What's going to happen to me now?"

"When we get back to town, Doc Evans can patch you up after he takes care of Jarrett." The lawman grabbed some of the bridles as he continued to speak. "You're spending the night in a jail cell. At daybreak you're riding out of town and never coming back. I'm giving you a second chance. Take advantage of it. Just because you're young doesn't mean you have to act like a fool kid."

A look of gratitude and relief filled Lenny's face. "Thanks, Sheriff. Thanks a lot."

"Come on. We've got work to do."

Riding one of Jarrett's fine wagons back to Gradyville, Matheson reckoned he would get a hold of Reverend Stubby upon arriving in town. The pastor would have to tell Mrs. Walter Jarrett that her husband was a crook and maybe a dying crook at that. She would take it hard. Maybell Jarrett was a fine woman, if a bit gullible. Matheson would suggest to the pastor that he encourage Maybell to appoint Ken Bradford, one of the bartenders at the Roman Holiday, to manage the place for her. Ken would do a fine job and wouldn't cheat Maybell.

Matheson shouted a giddyup to the team of horses in front of him, then laughed to himself. Well, he was certain Ken wouldn't cheat Maybell very much. In the West, you often had to make do.

The sheriff quickly glanced backward at the two horses tied to the wagon, then looked at the pale young man who was sitting beside him on the bench, half asleep. Matheson hoped he was doing the right thing.

Maybe a little time spent in jail would knock some sense into Lenny. But the kid seemed sensible enough, guilty primarily of being young. He would let him go in the morning and hope that he wouldn't become a problem for some other lawman somewhere down the trail.

Yeah, in the West, you often had to make do.

Chapter Seven

Boyd Matheson watched Lenny ride out of Gradyville, then headed to Dr. Rufus Evans' home. He knocked twice on the door, the second knock aimed at waking the sleeping doctor. The sheriff could hear a stirring inside. Doc Evans was slowly extricating himself from his easy chair. A rumpled, grouchy-looking man opened the door.

"I was hoping you'd bring me some breakfast."

Boyd managed a chuckle. "Haven't eaten yet myself. But I'll ask Hilda Flynn to bring you over a plate from the restaurant and—"

The doctor motioned Boyd into his living room, which also served as the waiting room for patients, then closed the door. "Tell her there's no rush. I'm not going anywhere."

Matheson looked at the doctor, who, like him, had

grabbed a few hours of sleep but hadn't found time to change his clothes. The doctor's salt-and-pepper hair was now predominantly salt. But the red veins on his nose were turning dull. Doc Evans had not had a drink for almost nine months. Having given up tobacco, Matheson figured that he could understand—some, anyway—what his friend was going through.

"No promises, Boyd, but I think Jarrett is going to make it." He nodded his head toward a closed door. "He's sleeping in my office right now. It could be a day or two before he's in any shape to talk."

"Could you wake him? I just want to ask—"

Rufus shook his head. "He couldn't tell you a thing in the condition he's in, and you would be risking his recovery."

Matheson sighed in reluctant agreement. "I get the point. I need Jarrett alive."

"From what you told me earlier, Jarrett was supply-ing the judge with a steady stream of cash. Last night you cut that stream off. I don't think the judge will take too kindly to that."

"Probably not." The sheriff looked about thoughtfully. "I'd better post a guard on this house. Those three hench-men who got away last night are back with their boss now. The judge knows that, dead or alive, we have Walter Jarrett. It won't take him long to find out Walter's alive. I don't want any problems here."

"What about you, Boyd? What about your problems? Do you have much medicine left?"

"Not too much."

"I'll drop some more by today."

"Thanks." Both Matheson and Doc Evans thought it a good idea for the sheriff not to be seen leaving the doc's place with a bottle of medicine in his hand. That might give encouragement to the wrong people. The problem was easy to solve, since Doc was frequently scooting about town with his black bag in tow. Occasionally he would stop by the sheriff's office and leave the medicine. Matheson lived in a room directly above the office.

"That cough of yours seems to be getting worse, Boyd. You need to start thinking about how—"

"Don't worry, I'm making plans."

"What kind of plans?"

"Can't go into all that now." The lawman walked hastily to the front door. "Need to get back to the office. Around here you never know what might happen next."

"That's true. You never know."

No one took much heed of the stranger who wandered into the Silver Creek Saloon that night. Gradyville was a prosperous town, and it wasn't unusual for newcomers to arrive looking for work. He called himself Clint Smith, a big man, heavyset but not fat. He was a friendly sort who didn't mind buying a round of drinks. Smith seemed interested in the town. He'd ask questions, then smile and listen carefully.

After a few hours at the Silver Creek, Clint strolled over to the Roman Holiday, where he got involved in a poker game. He threw in his cards around 2:00 A.M.

"I need to save some money for you fellas to win from me tomorrow night."

As Smith left the saloon, one of the men at the poker table remarked, "Nice fella. Hope he stays around."

Chapter Eight

Clint Smith moved through the darkness with an agility unusual for a man of his size. Thick clouds blanketed the moon. He was in luck, he thought, as he approached the house of Doc Evans. Clint Smith had cat eyes that could see well in the dark, and he figured that the old man he was about to attack was not so fortunate.

He stood behind a nearby tree and watched the house. The old man, the one some barflies had told him was named Hank Mellor, was standing on the porch, his eyes scanning the area. After a few minutes he left the porch and walked around the left side of the house.

Smith ran to the right side of the house and flattened himself against the wall. He could hear Hank's footsteps and weary sighs. Night watch could be pretty dull work.

Hank Mellor was seeing if he could spot anything untoward in the backyard as Smith peered around the corner of the house and took one step toward his prey.

"Who's there?"

Smith whispered a curse. He had underestimated the old man and gotten careless. Now he had to think fast.

"It's me, Pa—Orin." The men in the saloon had referred to Hank as Orin's "pa." He hoped the son used that same word.

Hank aimed his shotgun toward the voice. "You step toward me, real slow-like and careful."

Only a fool would have missed the suspicion in Hank's command, and Clint Smith was no fool. "Can't, Pa. I'm hurt bad."

Hank lowered his weapon and ran toward Clint Smith. Smith knew he had to move fast; the deception wouldn't last long. He jumped at Mellor and tackled him at the waist. Mellor dropped his shotgun and let out an "oomph" when he hit the ground. He had no time to say anything more. His attacker landed a hard punch against his left temple, which left him unconscious.

Smith pulled two bandannas from his back pocket and hastily gagged Hank Mellor and tied his hands. No need to worry about the old coot getting to his feet. The concussion and tied hands would slow him down considerably.

Satisfied that the guard would cause him no more problems, Clint pulled out a knife and pried open the back window of Doc Evans' house with a speed and skill honed over several years. He silently entered, holding on to the knife. For a moment he stood in the darkness, allowing his eyes to adjust. The intruder was standing in the portion of the doctor's house that he used for an office. On the left side of the office was a bed, where Jarrett lay recuperating from his gunshot wound. It really was amazing, the things a man could learn by keeping his ears open in a saloon for a few hours, Clint thought.

He walked to the door of the room and listened carefully. The doctor was snoring somewhere else in the house. Clint smiled and got to work.

Jarrett's clothes were folded by the bed where he lay, along with his boots. Only the saloon owner's shirt was missing; that had probably been thrown away because it was too blood soaked to have been of any more use. Clint looked down at the wounded crook as he tightened his grip on the knife. The man's left side was heavily bandaged, but his right arm was completely free. That could be a problem.

Jarrett's eyes opened, then widened in panic. Hovering over him was a face evincing the cold steel of a man who killed and enjoyed doing it. Clint slapped a hand over Jarrett's mouth, then jammed the knife into his chest. A cry of pain was smothered by the intruder's large hand; not until the body had gone limp did that hand lift.

Clint noted with some irritation that teeth marks now ran across his palm, though he found it funny that those marks were widely spread. That was Jarrett's problem, he mused to himself—the gent just had too big a mouth.

The killer left even more quietly than he had arrived.

Chapter Nine

Clint Smith felt nervous as he walked toward the boss' cabin in response to having his name called out. The judge was one strange hombre. According to the other men, Judge Cavanaugh seemed to know where every deserted cabin in the Arizona Territory was located, and the roof and four walls were always used by him alone. His gang had to sleep, play cards, and generally pass the time outdoors.

This cabin was a bit more shabby than the one they had abandoned yesterday; no porch here. Clint carefully kicked his boots against the front wall of the rickety structure before entering. The judge didn't like it when the underlings tracked dirt into his domain.

As Clint stepped inside, he noted that the judge was seated at a table with a lot of papers spread out in front of him, as he had been when Clint arrived two nights ago. What was on those papers? Clint had no idea.

"Sorry I can't offer you a chair." The judge's voice was friendly and his statement not surprising. There was only one chair in the cabin and never any doubt as to who would use it.

"I don't mind, Your Honor. Do my best thinking on my feet."

Judge Cavanaugh smiled at his new top henchman. "Is Clint your real name?"

"I never placed much importance on names, Judge," came the cautious reply. "Right now I'm Clint Smith. I've been Frank Bailey, Bill Jones, and a bunch of other names—pretty much forgotten what my ma really named me."

The judge laughed. "I'm a pipe man, myself"—he held up the object in his right hand—"but would you care for a cigar, Clint Smith?"

Smith said that he would but continued to feel a bit nervous. From what he had been told, the judge wasn't the kind of man who offered smokes to the hired hands. Clint lit his stogy and let the boss carry the conversation.

"Good to have you here, Clint. Too bad you arrived an hour or so too late to help out with that little raid we pulled in Gradyville on Wednesday—or tried to pull."

"I had another job to finish up, Your Honor."

The judge briefly pointed his pipe at Smith. "I understand that, and I respect you for it. We got ourselves a problem that needs to be straightened out quick."

"Don't worry, Judge. We'll get Russ out of jail, and—"

"Why?"

The question stunned Smith. "Well, uh—"

"What do you know about Sheriff Boyd Matheson?"

Clint had no trouble with that question. "From what I hear, he's fast and tough. Some say his deputy is almost as good."

"That's the reason we need to free that no-good boy of mine. And, believe me, he is a boy. Always will be." Cavanaugh stood up and opened the wooden shutters on the cabin's one small window, which was on the back wall. "Matheson's reputation is spreading throughout the Territory. If Russ is tried by a jury, I'll end up looking like a crook. We've got to free Russ and make Matheson look like a fool!—a fool who was outwitted by the Robin Hood of the Arizona Territory."

"Well . . ."

"Either people will believe that Matheson arrested a killer and brought him to justice, or they'll believe that Matheson arrested an innocent man and was bested by that man's father. Either we spend the rest of our lives in crummy shacks like this one, or we move into the governor's mansion."

Cavanaugh took several quick steps toward his henchman and spoke again when they were inches apart. "My plans have been blocked because I'm surrounded by fools—men who couldn't even disrupt a prayer meeting without getting killed and captured. You're different, Clint. Together we'll run Arizona. Look over the men we've got now. Keep the ones worth keeping, and get rid of the rest. Hire new men, tell them they'll be working for the governor someday."

Smith was astonished by the wildfire in the judge's eyes. This talk about being governor should have sounded like fool's talk, Clint thought to himself, but something in that wildfire made Clint believe it. "Sure, Your Honor. First we get Russ out of jail—"

"We've got to do more than that!" Cavanaugh began to pace about. "I can't be branded as a man who broke a killer out of jail—even if the killer is my son."

"But, Your Honor, you gave the town an ultimatum. Release Russ, or you would—"

"That was a bit of a mistake, but not a serious one. The plan failed, thanks to the buffoons who work for me. There is only one witness to my threat, the editor of the *Gradyville Gazette.* He can't do us too much harm. You know what kind of man gets power, real power, in the world, Clint?"

"No, Judge, guess I don't."

"A man who ascends to power is a man who sees beyond petty truths to the deeper truth and whose bigger truth is accepted by the people. Matheson must be made to look like a two-bit bully with a tin star. A lawdog who scapegoated Russ to make himself look good. I've got paid reporters who will help me get that story spread throughout the Territory." Cavanaugh's voice became a roar. "I intend to utterly destroy Matheson, the way he destroyed my prime source of money when he closed down Jarrett's operation! It'll take months to get something like that going again!"

Cavanaugh paused to calm his emotions. After a few moments of gazing at nothing he said, "Can you get the townspeople in Gradyville to turn on their sheriff? I don't care how you do it."

"Well, uh, sure. Guess folks are always willing to think the worst of someone else."

"Great. One way or another we'll get Russ out of jail and then kill him."

Judge Cavanaugh laughed at the astonished expression on his henchman's face. "My son has been an embarrassment to me all my life. Russ would just keep on doing everything wrong, dressing up like some circus performer and getting himself arrested. Best to bring it all to an end." He flicked his hand as if brushing away a small insect.

"But, Your Honor, all this talk about saving face. If Russ were to be killed, folks would think—"

"Hardly anybody will know. You'll become Russ Cavanaugh."

"Wha—"

The judge laughed again, and the wild blaze returned to his eyes. "Just tell folks in the next town we go to that you decided to get rid of the Buffalo Bill hair and beard. You've been Frank Bailey and Bill Jones. Well, I'll give you a name to be proud of, a name that will make you rich and powerful!"

Clint liked the idea of becoming Russ Cavanaugh, but for the first time since he was a boy, the gunman's hands trembled. Judge Lewis Rutherford Cavanaugh was not the kind of father a son should ever turn his back on.

Chapter Ten

Laurel Remick left the church feeling tense and apprehensive. She didn't know why. Reverend Steuben had been shocked and upset, as was only natural, but he still gave the advice she wanted to hear. Her small brown dog, Perkins, scampered beside her.

The young woman walked toward Remick's General Store, a store she helped her grandfather to run. She was a few minutes late; Clay would probably be waiting there.

Laurel did love Clay Adams. Of that, she was certain. Still, there was a confusion in her heart that only Reverend Steuben seemed to understand. Laurel had been attracted to Boyd Matheson from the moment he rode into Gradyville. She sensed that the sheriff was also attracted to her, but he would never admit it, because he believed that to do so would bring her a heap of misery.

As she stepped onto the boardwalk, Laurel wondered if Matheson's attitude didn't represent a very special form of love. She shook her head as if trying to dispel an idea she couldn't deal with at the moment. "I'll not think about what can't be," she said to her small companion.

Approaching the store, Laurel saw Clay standing on the boardwalk talking with her grandfather. Clay had struck up a real friendship with Cassius Remick, for which Laurel was grateful.

"So, you're finally back!" Cassius shouted to his grand-daughter, while bending over to pet the dog. "Guess you and the reverend have a lot more to talk about, what with the new piano and all. Takes more time to plan the Sunday services and other meetin's."

Laurel smiled at Cassius but said nothing. Talk about planning music had only taken a small fraction of her time with Reverend Steuben.

"You two get along to Flynn's Restaurant now. Enjoy yourselves, and don't let Harold Flynn bend your ears too much about how he was a lawman back in Texas."

"You really think Harold was a Texas Ranger, Cassius, and got his limp from a shootout with a gang of fourteen outlaws?" Clay laughed as he posed the question.

"Oh, I don't know. Harold sure is proud of that gun collection of his, likes to show it off, and he's good at shootin' away old cans, but the important thing is that he and Hilda are mighty fine cooks. Now, you two get to your supper." Cassius waved a hand as if shooing the couple in the direction of the restaurant.

"Grandfather, I left that stew for you—"

Cassius' hand became more animated. "Thanks, and

stop worryin'. Just move along. Perkins, you come with me."

The old man retreated into the store. Perkins gave his mistress a mournful look. "Go with Grandpa." The dog reluctantly obeyed. Laurel and Clay joined hands and began to walk toward the restaurant.

"Clay, would it be all right if we strolled in the direction of the church before eating? I know I just came from there, but I'd like to walk a bit more to work up an appetite."

"My appetite is worked up plenty, but, sure, I'd enjoy a walk." Clay's voice was casual, but he suspected that his fiancée had something important to say and wanted some quiet to say it in. There was a stretch of nothing much between the boardwalk and the church—the perfect location for a private talk.

"How's Hank doing?" Laurel asked while they were still on the boardwalk.

"Pretty good." Clay gave his fiancée a crooked grin. "He's a tough old bird. Says he'll be back in action tomorrow, and I believe him."

"Do you have any idea who murdered Walter Jarrett?" Laurel spoke as they stepped off the boardwalk.

The smile vanished from Clay's face. "No. We don't know who actually did the killing. Boyd thinks Judge Cavanaugh ordered Jarrett killed because he might have told us something that would help us locate that whole bunch. I think the sheriff's right."

They walked under a mesquite tree and stopped there. Laurel spoke in a low voice. "Clay, you must do everything you can to help Sheriff Matheson."

The deputy shrugged. "Of course. That's my job—"

"Clay, Sheriff Matheson is dying."

"What! What do you mean?" Clay shouted his words, then hastily looked around as Laurel shushed him. No one was near.

"A while back, I overheard Dr. Evans talking to the sheriff." Laurel continued to speak quietly. "They didn't know I was nearby. The doctor told Sheriff Matheson that he didn't have long to live—six months, maybe a year or two. I told the sheriff about what I heard and promised him I'd tell no one else. I didn't keep my promise. I just now told Reverend Steuben, and I asked him if I should tell you. He said that I should. But we're the only ones who know."

"There's nothing the doc can do?"

"Dr. Evans told the sheriff to give up tobacco. He did, and that has helped some but, no, there's nothing . . ."

"I have noticed that cough of his getting worse—" Clay saw that his fiancée was crying and gently enveloped her in his arms. As he held her, Adams thought that now was the time to ask questions that had been causing him to worry. But then, maybe some things were best just left unspoken.

No. He had to ask. Clay released the young woman as she began to compose herself. He kissed her gently on the forehead. "Laurel, I've noticed that you and Boyd—I mean, you've never done anything wrong, nothing like that, but, sometimes, well, you sort of look at each other in a special way. If Boyd hadn't've been sick—"

"Clay," Laurel hastily interrupted. "Have you ever

been out riding and spotted a trail off to the side and wondered where that trail led to?"

The deputy shrugged his shoulders. "Sure. Happens all the time. But I can't think on it too much. Never get anything done."

"I'm the same way," Laurel said softly. "I wonder where a trail would have led. But I don't think on it too much because I've decided which trail I am taking. I love you, Clay, and I don't want to share my life with anyone else but you. Life has been so good to us, but it's not that way for Boyd Matheson. I want to do everything I can for Mr. Matheson, even though it won't amount to much, and I know you feel the same way I do."

"I owe Boyd Matheson a lot. I wasn't much more than a two-bit crook when he made me his deputy. Don't worry, I'll help him. I'll do everything I can."

"I know you will."

They joined hands again and walked back toward the town. Clay Adams stopped worrying about his relationship with his fiancée and started to think on her statement about life not being very kind to Boyd Matheson. From time to time Clay uttered a curse under his breath, and Laurel nodded in agreement.

Chapter Eleven

The man who called himself Clint Smith rode confidently toward the Johnstone ranch house. The sun was beginning to hang at eye level. Smith figured that Ezra would be inside his house but with a chunk of time to pass before supper. He stopped his horse in front of a hitch rail. "Hello, the house!"

A young, dark-haired girl of fourteen stepped onto the porch. She was a pretty thing, Smith thought, with a button nose and green eyes. The girl had an apron tied at her waist. Her smile was tentative but still carried a lot of charm.

She never got to speak. A young man—obviously her brother, by his coloring and facial features—stepped onto the porch in front of her. A stranger could mean trouble, and this was man's work. "Good afternoon." The boy's voice squeaked a bit; it was changing. Smith pegged his age at fifteen or sixteen.

"Good afternoon." Smith touched his hat with two fingers and nodded politely at the girl. "I know this is the Johnstone ranch, and a fine spread it is." He turned to the boy. "You must be Jim Johnstone."

Jimmy Johnstone smiled. He liked being called Jim instead of Jimmy.

"That's right, and I'm Ezra." The old man spoke as he stepped onto the porch. "If you're looking for work, stranger, you'll have to talk with my foreman, Ned Myers."

"It's not work I'm looking for Mr. Johnstone, just a little conversation."

"What about?"

"Your oldest son, Zack."

"What about Zack?"

"This is sort of private, Mr. Johnstone. If I could speak to you alone for a few minutes . . ."

Ezra couldn't refuse the request. The stranger might know something that could help Zack. Besides, it would be a relief to talk openly about the one thing he had been thinking about since that awful day the deputy arrived with the news.

"Come on in."

"Obliged."

Clint dismounted, hastily tied his horse to the hitching rail, then trailed the three Johnstones into the house. "Pa, would you and our guest like some coffee?" Ezra's daughter, Esther, spoke for the first time.

"The young lady has made a very kind offer, Mr. Johnstone. But, no, thank you, I won't be staying long. You are busy folks. I won't take much of your time."

Ezra nodded. "Esther, why don't you get back to helping fix supper? Jim, I think Ned needs your help."

The two young people immediately obeyed their father but did so with a touch of resentment. Since their mother's death they had taken over many adult responsibilities. They felt insulted by being excluded from an important meeting as if they were still children.

Ezra sensed how his children felt and made a mental note to make it up to them later. "Please sit down, Mr.—"

"Smith. Clint Smith. There's something else you should know about me." He pulled an Arizona Rangers badge from his shirt pocket, then returned it there. The skepticism that had been evident on Ezra's face vanished. Strange, what a six-pointed star could do to people, Smith mused. He had long forgotten the name of the Ranger whose shirt he had ripped the badge from, though he did recall ambushing the lawman with a sawed-off scattergun from behind a large cottonwood.

"Most Arizona Rangers I know wear their badges where folks can see it." Johnstone smiled and motioned his guest toward an armchair. Ezra sat in a large rocking chair, facing the bogus Ranger.

Clint Smith chuckled softly. "So do I, sir, most of the time, but I am on a very unusual job right now."

"What might that be?"

"Well, as you know, Mr. Johnstone, the Arizona Rangers sometimes take over the law in a town where the sheriff is corrupt or incompetent."

"Yes, but Boyd Matheson is an honest man—"

"Matheson is a man of integrity, but you, better than anyone in Gradyville, know that he is not handling this situation with Judge Cavanaugh's gang very well."

An anger that had been flowing inside Ezra Johnstone suddenly erupted. " 'Not handling it well' is putting it mildly, don't you think? Boyd Matheson has my boy in a place where he could easily get killed!"

Smith looked toward the ceiling in an all-knowing manner, then returned his gaze to the old man. "That's why the Rangers need to get Matheson out of that sheriff's office, fast as lightning."

"How can you do that?"

Clint Smith paused for a moment. This was the hardest part of his lawman's charade, and it had to be good. Smith folded his hands and looked intensely into Ezra's eyes; two men of the world discussing how things sometimes had to be.

"Mr. Johnstone, maintaining justice is hard and sometimes pretty complicated. We don't like it, but the Arizona Rangers, now and again, have to break the law in order to maintain justice."

"Well, yes, I understand."

"Gradyville has a serious problem. Boyd Matheson is a good small-town sheriff. But that's all he is. He can't deal with a problem like Judge Cavanaugh. The Rangers need to take control of the town until the whole Cavanaugh matter is done away with. Then Matheson can have his job back."

"I still can't fathom how you can do such a thing."

Smith smiled sadly, a man saddled with life's unfair burdens. "The Rangers have faced situations like this before, sir. Our answer has been to stage crimes in the town—"

"What!"

"Yes, Mr. Johnstone. We don't like it, but, by creating chaos, we get a large number of local citizens to request that the Rangers intervene. That's necessary before we can do anything. Sometimes we don't have enough men to pull it off ourselves; that's when we need help from people like yourselves."

"You expect me to commit a crime?" Ezra's voice was a near shout.

"If you want your son to live, yes."

Ezra fell silent. Confusion dominated his tired, bloodshot eyes.

Clint Smith spoke in a kind but persistent voice. "All I need is two men, to rob the stage depot tomorrow." He pulled a hand-drawn map from a side pocket and handed it to the rancher. "The men will meet me up in the mountains. I'll be with another Ranger. I know the area. It's almost impossible to track anyone there."

"What happens after that?"

"We give the money to my Ranger friend. He rides into town and returns the money to the stage depot with a story about how he spotted the outlaws and got the cash away from them even though they managed to escape."

"Meantime my men return here and keep their mouths shut."

Clint's smile became approving. "Right. There have

been plenty of problems in Gradyville lately. I suspect that with this robbery tomorrow, the Rangers will be in charge of the town real soon."

"But, wait, tomorrow is Sunday."

"Yes, and that makes it all the easier. Every Sunday Howard Lowry stops by the depot at about dawn to get some paperwork done before he goes to church. We need Lowry to open the safe. Most of the town will be deserted at that time on a Sunday morning. The stage depot will be easy pickin's." Clint Smith again smiled to himself as he reflected on all that he had learned by listening to men jaw in a saloon.

There was a brief period of silence, which Smith broke. "Of course, once the Rangers take over the town, our top priority will be to get Zack out of jail."

"I know a man who can handle the job, and he can choose a good partner. Let's talk to him right now." The confusion was gone from Ezra Johnstone's eyes, replaced by determination. He would do whatever was necessary to protect his boy.

Chapter Twelve

Joel Hogan stood nervously in the alley and looked up at the red streaks in the sky. Howard Lowry should be along soon, if he was keeping to his usual schedule, which folks in town said that he always did.

"Ain't this somethin'?" Tommy Skerrit whispered to his partner. He was holding a rope and a heavy piece of cloth. "Us robbin' the stage depot to help the Arizona Rangers? I'll bet that Kibler fella will want to write somethin' 'bout us in that paper of his. There might even be a book 'bout us. Can't wait til Esther knows."

"Would you forget about that girl? Old man Johnstone would run you out of the Territory if he knowed that you was spooning with her."

"Old man Johnstone's got nothin' to say about—"

"Okay, okay." Tommy was just a kid of sixteen. Joel knew that, at eighteen, he had to provide the cool head. "Quiet, someone's comin'."

True to his reputation, Howard Lowry was walking down the boardwalk, softly humming a hymn. He stopped at the stage depot, unlocked the front door, and left the door open so that what little light came from outside could guide him to his desk.

Something about hearing a familiar hymn increased Joel's nervousness. He cautiously stepped out of the alley and looked around. The town appeared empty. He motioned for Tommy to follow him. Both men hastily moved their bandannas onto their faces and entered the stage depot. As Tommy closed the door, Joel drew his gun. "Open the safe, or I'll kill you."

A look of terror came across Lowry's face, highlighted by the kerosene glow from the desk lamp he had just lit. Howard Lowry was a tall, thin man with the whitest skin Joel had ever seen. How did the guy stay the color of milk in the Arizona Territory, the ranch-hand wondered to himself.

"There's not much money there right now." The tremble in Howard's voice and body reminded Joel that he needed to keep his mind on the job at hand.

"Ain't nobody gonna have money in their safe before long." Tommy walked briskly toward Lowry, tossed the rope and cloth onto the desk, and waved his gun in a threatening manner. Joel became frightened. That fool kid might accidentally shoot Lowry. "Open that safe. Do what we tell ya," Tommy barked.

As Howard moved toward the safe, footsteps could be heard from outside. Joel motioned for Tommy to crouch down behind the desk, as he flattened himself against the wall beside the front door.

Cletus Browning, one of the stage line's drivers, strolled into the office. "Mornin', Howard. Needed to stop by a moment to—"

Joel Hogan quickly advanced on the stagecoach driver and smashed his six-gun against the back of Browning's head. The driver gave a yelp, then dropped to the floor, where he rolled about and moaned in a loud voice.

Joel was confused and panicked. In all the dime novels he had read, characters who got their skulls banged always dropped over unconscious. Maybe Cletus had a harder head than most.

"Shut up, ya old cuss, or I'll kill ya!" Hogan ordered in a loud whisper. He glanced at the other two men. Howard continued to look terrified; his hands were high in the air. Tommy was standing back up, his eyes now confused and frightened.

"Get that safe open—quick!" Hogan motioned with his gun toward the safe.

"Yeah!" Tommy tried to sound tough as he shoved the manager toward the safe.

Joel hastily untied Cletus' bandanna and stuffed it into his mouth. The old coot was quiet now but looking at him carefully. Joel had been in a couple of card games with Cletus, but the two men didn't really know each other well. Still, Joel made a note not to come into town for a while unless Cletus was gone on a run.

Hogan yanked the belt from Cletus' pants and used it to tie the stage driver's hands. He figured his handiwork would hold for about ten minutes, no longer, that was for certain.

"Here's the money!" Tommy ran toward the back door, waving a canvas bag. "Let's git!"

"No, T—" Joel had almost used his partner's name. "We have to tie up the manager."

"Oh, yeah."

Howard Lowry obeyed the instructions the two bogus outlaws gave him to lie down and not resist as they tied him up with the rope and used the cloth to gag his mouth. Still, Joel wondered if both Howard and Cletus might begin to suspect that they were being held up by the stupidest crooks in the Arizona Territory.

Joel and Tommy ran out the back door of the stage depot to where their horses were waiting for them.

Several hours later, the two make-believe thieves were relaxing by a mountain stream while their horses drank. "Been a hard ride," Joel said to his younger companion. "But the Ranger was right. Nobody can track us up here."

Tommy placed his newly filled canteen back onto his saddle. "You and me are gonna be heroes once news 'bout what we done gits out. Bet that Esther will want me to become a lawdog of some kind. But I think I'll stick with ranchin'. How 'bout you?"

Joel smiled in agreement. "I'm stickin' with ranchin'. Hope to have my own spread someday." Still, Joel did admit privately to himself that he would enjoy it when everyone learned that he and Tommy had committed a robbery to help the Arizona Rangers.

After another fifteen minutes or so of such talk both men mounted their horses and continued the long, twisting ride. As they rode up a narrow trail toward a plateau,

Joel spotted two men. "There they are!" he shouted jubi-
lantly. "Right where the map said they would be."

The bogus thieves were jovial as they reached the
plateau and shouted out friendly greetings to Clint Smith.
But as they dismounted, Joel became a bit tense. The man
with Smith sure didn't look like an Arizona Ranger. He
was a lot older than Clint and dressed pretty fancy. But
then, maybe he was a boss man of some kind.

"Hello, fellas. How'd it go?" Clint was standing by a
small campfire, a cup in hand. A pot of coffee hung
over the fire, but he didn't offer the new arrivals any.

"Went good, Clint." Joel spoke in a friendly manner.

"Did anybody see your faces, be able to identify
you?" Clint placed his cup down on a tree stump.

Joel didn't like the cold, distant sound of Smith's
voice. He shrugged his shoulders as he approached the
campfire. "No, Clint. Like I said, everything went good."

Tommy didn't sense the absence of friendliness. He
stepped quickly toward the campfire, a bag dangling
from one hand. "You shoulda seen the look on Howard
Lowry's face when we busted in. You can sure bet he'll
be grateful when you fellas return—"

"How much money did you get?" The fancy-dressed
man snatched the sack away from Tommy.

"Me and Joel didn't have time to count it. But we
think it's about four hunnert."

"Those are good horses." The older man nodded toward their steeds. Tommy and Joel briefly turned their
heads to look at the horses. When they turned back
around, Clint Smith was holding a gun in his right hand.
He quickly pumped two bullets into each man.

Joel staggered, then dropped to the ground. A buzzing noise filled his ears. He could hear the fancy-dressed man say something about burying people and Clint needing to hurry back to town. Then he detected a low whimpering and heard Tommy crying for Esther. For a moment, Joel felt angry at Tommy and then turned the anger on himself. Tommy was just a kid, but he was a grown man. He should somehow have stopped this from happening.

That thought tore through him as he fought for his last breath.

Chapter Thirteen

Ezra Johnstone looked around his large barn. He had helped his brother to build it many years ago, and for some reason the place always gave him a sense of pride and well-being. Not today. Esther and Jim had returned from church with a story about the stage depot being robbed and Cletus Browning being assaulted by one of the crooks. From what Ezra could garner, the stage-coach driver would be all right. Still, Cletus was no frisky colt. A smash on the skull could have . . .

The rancher looked at the two horses his own son had stolen in order to help a couple of no-good thieves. What had gotten into Zack? And why hadn't Joel and his partner returned yet?

Johnstone strode out of the barn, trying to think about the Sunday dinner that would be ready in an hour or so. Clint Smith was standing outside. At first, the rancher was elated, but something in Smith's eyes drained any good feeling out of Ezra.

"Why don't you step back into the barn, Mr. Johnstone? We need to talk."

Ezra shrugged his shoulders. "We can talk out here."

"That's not such a good idea, Mr. Johnstone." A smirk spread across Smith's face. "I don't think you'd want a passing cowhand to hear that his boss is a thief."

"What are you talking about?"

Clint pointed toward the barn. "Inside."

Ezra obeyed, feeling humiliated to be given orders on his own ranch. "What's this all about?" he demanded as the two men stood alone in the barn.

"Jim and Esther already have a big brother in jail. You wouldn't want their papa to be joining him, would you?"

"What—"

"You ordered two of your men to rob the stage depot, Mr. Johnstone. I have a written confession, signed by Joel Hogan, which names you as the boss of the whole operation." Smith patted the front pocket of his shirt, which, in fact, contained a blank piece of paper.

"Only to help the Arizona Rangers!"

Clint Smith gave a loud laugh. "Who would believe that?"

Ezra Johnstone closed his eyes and clenched his fists. An unspoken fear that he had carried inside him for almost twenty-four hours had just been realized. When he opened his eyes, they were filled with defeat and resignation. "You're not really a Ranger, are you." It wasn't really a question.

This time Clint's laugh was even more mocking than before.

"Where are Joel and Tommy?"

"All in good time, Mr. Johnstone. The first thing you've got to remember is that from now on, you don't ask any questions, you only take orders. And it won't be so bad. Just do what I tell you, and that boy of yours will be out of jail before the sheriff gets him killed."

Ezra looked at the ground and said nothing.

"You're going into politics, Mr. Johnstone. Getting folks to sign a petition."

"What kind of petition?"

Clint took two quick steps toward the rancher and placed a hard finger on his chest. "I said you don't ask any more questions, got it?" He shoved Ezra backward a few steps, then walked toward the barn doors. He turned abruptly and viewed the rancher with hard, threatening eyes. "I'll overlook it this time, Mr. Johnstone, but don't make that mistake again."

Clint Smith departed, and Ezra was once again alone in a barn that he had helped to build. But the feeling of comfort and well-being was gone forever.

"Are you sure you don't want a piece of apple pie, Father?" Esther asked as she gathered up the dishes from the dinner table.

"No, thanks. I'm just not very hungry this afternoon."

Esther had actually baked the pie with Tommy in mind. She had planned to take him a piece after the family had eaten. Jim, who was still seated at the table, asked the question she had been worrying over for the last few hours.

"When are Joel and Tommy getting back, Father? Joel is going to help me fix that—"

"Get someone else. I don't know when they'll be back."

Jim looked confused. His father didn't usually talk that way. "What kind of errand did you send them on, anyway?"

"Nothing important." Ezra's voice took on a new force. Was it anger, frustration, or something else? The two young Johnstones had never seen their father act this way before.

"But they've got to get back soon," Jim persisted, "unless they're going to make camp somewhere—"

"You know how ranch hands are. They get itchy feet." Ezra flitted a hand back and forth, trying to look casual and not succeeding. "They may be gone for days, weeks—who knows?"

"Tommy isn't like that!" Esther wailed.

Jim shot a look of caution at his sister. He would handle this. "Sis has a point, Father. Joel and Tommy are two of the most reliable men we've got. If they haven't come back, maybe we'd better—"

"I don't want to hear any more about this!" Ezra Johnstone slammed a fist onto the table. "Both of you have chores to do. Now get to it!"

Esther's face contorted as she hurried from the dining room. Moments after she entered the kitchen, there was the sound of crying. Jim left the table and followed his sister. Ezra could hear his son trying to comfort the girl. "Father isn't himself right now. Everything is going to be fine. . . ."

Everything wasn't going to be fine, and Ezra knew it. A shudder ran through him as, for the first time, he allowed himself to wonder whether Joel and Tommy were still alive. The rancher grabbed a napkin from the table and quickly dabbed his eyes. He had only wanted to protect his oldest son. But Ezra Johnstone had stepped over a line and become a different man. He knew that he could never turn back.

Chapter Fourteen

Reverend Stubby closed his Bible and his eyes. His brief prayer brought him one of the few peaceful moments he had experienced that day. He stood up from the desk in his small living quarters and checked his pocket watch. The Sunday evening service was less than an hour away.

He stepped into the sanctuary of the church and onto the platform where Laurel Remick was practicing on the piano. "Sounds wonderful." Reverend Stubby spoke without exaggeration.

"Thank you." Laurel smiled and stopped playing. She could tell that the pastor wanted to talk.

"Laurel, did you notice anything unusual about the service this morning?"

"No, not offhand."

"We had some new people attending."

Laurel turned up the smile a bit. "I'm sure the Lord guided them here."

"I'm not." The clergyman's reply was abrupt. "There were some strange things going on. Before and after the service, I noticed people huddling together as if they were sharing some kind of secret."

"Now that you mention it, there did seem to be a lot of whispering back and forth. What do you think it was about?"

"Well, Laurel, one of my professors from back East would say that the congregation was no doubt preparing to announce that they had received word from on high that God was calling me to a new ministry and request that I prayerfully consider where I should go next. That's a common way church folks have of getting rid of their pastor."

Laurel picked up on the levity in Reverend Stubby's voice. "Come on, we could never replace you."

"You're right," the pastor replied with mock serious-ness. "Where else would they find a man of my integrity, dedication, and learnedness? Besides, I work cheap."

They shared a chuckle, then Laurel said, "You're re-ally bothered by what happened this morning."

The clergyman nodded. "I hope you're right. I hope the Lord guided those new folks to our church. But I don't think so. I think there was evil in our church this morning. Real evil."

Laurel Remick inhaled, and tension gripped her. This time Reverend Stubby wasn't joking.

* * *

As the pastor finished his brief sermon, he carefully scanned the congregation. The strangers were once again in attendance: three of them, all men. Of course, they could be new in town, looking for work. Still . . .

Reverend Stubby stepped to the side of the pulpit. "I notice that we have some visitors in church tonight. I believe that you were also here this morning. I'm sorry that I didn't have a chance to meet you earlier." The last statement was a polite polishing of the truth. He had tried to meet them, but the men had avoided him.

"Perhaps I should explain how things work in this service. On Sunday nights my sermon is short. Though not short enough, some would say." There was light laughter, then the clergyman continued. "After the message, we open it up and allow anyone who is here to stand and give a testimony. Who would like to be first, this evening?"

There were a few testimonies from people who had a loved one bedridden by sickness or a serious accident and wanted to thank God and their neighbors for helping them through a difficult time. Reverend Stubby believed firmly that it was good for people to speak out on such matters. Openness helped bring the town together. The pastor was starting to feel less anxious.

Ezra Johnstone stood up. This was the first time Ezra had spoken in the evening service since he thanked everyone for their help during his wife's illness. Reverend Stubby noted that, contrary to his usual habit of sitting in the back, Ezra was now seated in a second pew from the front. One of the strangers was sitting beside him. Ezra's two younger children were not present. The pastor's anxiety returned.

"Reverend, we all know that our town has been through a series of horrible calamities. A bank clerk was shot down in cold blood, and most of the gang that was responsible are still free as birds. Innocent people, including a woman and children, were shot down in front of this church. And—what do you know?—most of the killers escaped. A short while later, Walter Jarrett was murdered. From what I hear, our sheriff has no idea who did it. Only yesterday, the stage depot was robbed. I'd say that Gradyville is a town in desperate need of decent law enforcement!"

A flurry of words spread across the sanctuary. By the differing tones of voices, Reverend Stubby could tell that people were strongly divided in their loyalties. He quickly held up both hands. "I will remind everyone that this is not a town meeting. This is a wor—" His eyes fell on Boyd Matheson, who was motioning for him not to stop Ezra from speaking. Stubby reluctantly went along with the sheriff's request. "This is a worship service, but I understand the need for folks to discuss some of the terrible events we have gone through together. Go ahead, Ezra."

The rancher's hand trembled noticeably as he reached into the pocket of his suit coat and pulled out two pieces of paper. "Reverend, I have here a petition signed by one hundred and six citizens of this town—that's six more than necessary—demanding that Gradyville have an election for the office of sheriff within ten days."

Several gasps, a few laughs, and a lot of chatter

followed Ezra's remark. Beau Kibler, who was sitting in a back pew, instinctively yanked a pen and note-book from his suit pocket and began to take notes.

Reverend Stubby again held up his hands for silence. "Ezra, as you know, our sheriff, Boyd Matheson, was not elected. He was appointed by the town council at a time when Gradyville faced a severe crisis. At the council meeting last week, it was decided, with Sheriff Matheson's approval, that the office of sheriff would become an elected office. The first election will be held in one year."

Ezra raised his voice to a shout. "I'd say that our town is facing a terrible crisis right now! We can't wait one year." He left his pew, dramatically strutted down the aisle, and handed the clergyman the petition. "Mr. Mayor, do your duty!" He turned in a huff and paraded back to his pew, receiving some applause and a scatter-ing of cheers.

Beau Kibler cringed as he furiously took notes. In his newspaper article on the last town meeting, he had written about a rule that was passed regarding a citi-zen's right to ask for an unscheduled election. The council had regarded it as mostly a technical matter, not of much importance. It was turning out to be very im-portant indeed.

Reverend Stubby scanned the petition and was shocked by some of the names on it. However, the sig-natures all looked genuine. "Very well," the pastor said. "Tomorrow, anyone who wishes to run—"

Ezra Johnstone quickly sprang to his feet. Stubby tried to contain his own frustration. Once again the church was the scene of an ambush, this one being car-ried out under the guise of civic duty. "Yes, Ezra."

"We don't have to wait until tomorrow, Mr. Mayor." He nodded at the man seated next to him. "I would like to introduce everyone to Mr. Clint Smith."

Smith stood up hurriedly as Ezra sat down. He knew that the man's nervous, huffy attitude had irritated many people, and he set about to smooth that situation over. His voice was friendly and informal. "Thank you, Mr. Johnstone, but, looking around here, I see that you don't have to introduce me to everyone. Some of you men know why I am running for sheriff. I need the work. You took all my money at the card table."

The laughter was stopped by the iron in Reverend Stubby's voice. "Mr. Smith, you are a newcomer to Gradyville. Why are you so interested in running for sheriff in a town that you know nothing about?"

"That's a good question, Preacher. Thanks for asking it." Clint Smith cast a quick glance around the church. "I am proud to declare before everyone here that I am representing Judge Lewis Rutherford Cavanaugh."

A loud commotion followed Smith's declaration. Reverend Stubby waved his hands and tried to shout over the loud talk. He saw, through the open door, Orin Mellor standing outside with his shotgun. Yes, they had posted a guard, and most of the men had come to church armed that night. But evil had still worked its way into the church like a snake slithering into a garden.

Boyd Matheson was sitting in a back pew. He ex-changed glances with his deputy, who was sitting beside Cassius Remick at the end of a middle pew. Clay had arrived at the church with Laurel and her grandfather and would be leaving with them. Matheson avoided Clay and the Remicks while in church. As he saw it, church was a place where Clay, Laurel, and her grandfather were together as a family. He didn't belong to that family and needed to keep his distance.

The sheriff got up and moved as inconspicuously as he could down the left aisle of the church and placed a hand on his deputy's shoulder as he whispered, "This could get out of hand. Smith's got two other gunmen with him here tonight."

"I see them," Adams shot back quickly.

"We need to stand at the front, where we can watch everyone. But let's do it nice and quiet." The two lawmen walked directly to the platform and stepped onto it, Matheson on the left side and Adams on the right. Since the choir loft behind them was empty on Sunday night, the two men now had an unobstructed view of everyone in the church.

"Mr. Smith." The pastor spoke after the actions of the lawmen had restored order. "How can you run for sheriff while being connected with one of the most vicious gangs of thieves and killers to ever ride across the Arizona Territory? Were you a part of the gang that attacked this church?"

"No, Preacher, and Judge Cavanaugh had nothing to do with it!" Clint Smith again looked over the crowd. "There have been a lot of lies told about Judge Cavanaugh lately. I'm here to tell the truth. The judge got tired of seeing powerful criminals go free because they could afford a high-priced lawyer. He got fed up with the law and decided that he cared more about justice!"

There was a scattering of cheers. Boyd Matheson glanced across the platform at his deputy. Clay Adams' face was red with anger. Matheson had talked a lot with Clay about keeping his temper in check. Tonight, he'd find out whether those talks did any good.

"Judge Cavanaugh has broken some laws here and there," Smith continued. "But he does it to help widows, orphans, and other folks who need help. This has made Judge Cavanaugh a lot of enemies. The kind of enemies who will hire a gang of hard cases to shoot down innocent folks in front of a church and blame it on the judge."

Laurel Remick was sitting at the piano, stunned by the positive response that Smith was getting from a good portion of the congregation. "You say that Judge Cavanaugh is concerned about widows and orphans, Mr. Smith. Did he teach that concern to his son? Thanks to Russ Cavanaugh, Elaine Jensen is a widow, and her two kids have no father. Russ saw to that when he gunned down Rollie Jensen while robbing the bank."

Laurel's remark received a louder, more positive response from the crowd than anything Clint Smith had said. The gunman knew he had to recover quickly. "Excuse me, ma'am, but I've always believed a man to be innocent until proven otherwise."

"That matter will be taken care of when the circuit judge arrives!"

There was a chorus of cheers. The young lady at the piano was winning over the crowd. Clint Smith had to recover lost ground. "I think this town is in for a big surprise when that circuit judge arrives."

Smith stepped out of the pew and into the center aisle to better address the crowd. "Russ Cavanaugh was camping out a few miles northwest of Gradyville when two riders approached the camp. They asked for grub. Russ could see that something wasn't right. He started asking questions, and, before you know it, a fight broke out. Russ had to kill both men. He inspected their saddlebags and found the money. Russ did what a son of Lewis Rutherford Cavanaugh would do. He started to ride into Gradyville to return the cash."

Clint's face suddenly became grim. "But on the way, he encountered your sheriff and his deputy. He told them his name and turned the money over to them."

Clint turned toward the platform, slowly stared at the two lawmen standing there, then looked back at the congregation. "But the two lawdogs wanted some glory for themselves. They beat Russ up and brought him in as a prisoner with some fool tale about the son of the famous Judge Cavanaugh holding up the bank. I'll bet one of the first things they did was run to the newspaper office with a tale of what heroes they were. Now, you folks understand why the judge is so outraged! Why he demands that his son be set free at once!"

Cheers sounded once again for Clint Smith. Beau Kibler thought about the many people who saw Boyd Matheson come to the newspaper office that day and bring him to the sheriff's office. But Matheson's purpose had been to give the reporter a full story about the money being recovered and returned to the bank.

The iron in Reverend Stubby's voice hardened. "You have made some very serious accusations, sir. Do you have any evidence to back it up?"

"That evidence will be presented where it should, Preacher—in court. Meanwhile, if elected sheriff, I will release Russ Cavanaugh and Zack Johnstone until the circuit judge arrives."

A wave of applause was stopped by Laurel Remick's voice. "And what if you are not elected, Mr. Smith? Will Judge Cavanaugh destroy this town as he has threatened to do if his boy is not released?"

"Don't believe everything you read in the newspaper, ma'am, especially some newspapers." Clint Smith looked accusingly at Beau Kibler, who shot back a hard stare. Smith then returned his gaze to the congregation. He knew that he had won over some converts, but not enough. Something powerful and shocking was needed. The gunman took a huge gamble.

"Yep, despite some of the stuff you read in the *Gradyville Gazette,* Judge Cavanaugh is a good man who cares for this town. And before this election is over, Judge Cavanaugh will appear right here in Gradyville and talk to you himself."

This time, Reverend Stubby waited a couple of minutes before he even tried to quiet the crowd. When order was restored, Clay Adams was the first to speak. The deputy's face was still red with anger, but his voice held at a steady monotone. "Mr. Smith, if that is your real name, I want you to know that we could arrest you right now. From what you say, you have some knowledge that could help us apprehend a wanted man. But we won't

do that. Boyd Matheson and I try to uphold the spirit of
the law, not just the letter of the law."

"Well, that's mighty nice of you, Deputy. Not tossing
your competition behind bars. I'll say this for the lawdogs around here, they're polite."

The chorus of laughs didn't inflame Adams' temper.
His voice remained calm. "If Judge Cavanaugh rides
into town, we may not be so polite. Your boss has been
involved in robberies where men were killed. We'll arrest him for murder."

Clint Smith laughed mockingly. "Judge Cavanaugh
isn't worried about getting arrested, Deputy. He knows
what kind of law enforcement this town is stuck with
right now. In fact, the judge asked me and some of my
friends here if we could help out even before the election.
So we went after the thieves who pulled a recent holdup."

The gunman took a few dramatic steps back to the pew
where he had been sitting and picked up a set of saddlebags. He then walked slowly across the aisle to Howard
Lowry, who was sitting in a front pew. "Mr. Lowry, this
belongs to you. It is the money that was stolen from the
stage depot. The thieves put up a fight, and we had to kill
them. Guess that's just as well. The jails in Gradyville
seem to be filling up with innocent people."

Howard Lowry stood up, took the saddlebags, and
shook Smith's hand, as laughter and applause spread
across the church. Smith smiled at the congregation, then
shouted out, "That's all I got to say right now. Looking
forward to meeting all of you this week!" He returned to
his pew and once again sat down beside Ezra Johnstone.

Reverend Stubby was angry with just about everyone,

especially himself. He had allowed the service to get completely out of hand. The pastor tried to keep the anger from his voice as he spoke. "Since this time of worship seems to have turned into a political rally, I feel that I should allow Sheriff Matheson an opportunity to speak in his defense."

"I think there's been enough speech-making tonight, Reverend." Matheson spoke softly. "Folks here know how I do my job. They can vote as they see fit."

"Thank you, Sheriff." Stubby paused. Boyd Matheson wouldn't brag on himself, and the clergyman wondered if he should say something in the lawman's favor. He decided against it. "As mayor of this town, I hereby call an election for sheriff to be held one week from tomorrow. As pastor of this church, I now call for a time of prayer. I think this town very much needs it."

Chapter Fifteen

Boyd Matheson stood over the coffeepot in the sheriff's office and inhaled the steam that shot up from the boiling water. Doc Evans had told him that this act could clear the lungs a bit, and Matheson believed that it worked. At least, it worked better than the medicine the doctor gave him. Doc Evans had expressed doubt as to whether the medicine was really effective, but they both agreed that it was worth a try.

Matheson laughed bitterly into the steam as he thought about how the church meeting last night had changed his life. Yes, he had agreed with the town council that the sheriff should be elected. But he had planned to announce his retirement toward the end of the year and allow Clay Adams to run for sheriff. "Guess life just can't be that nice and neat," he said aloud.

The lawman retrieved some beans and began to make coffee. He couldn't step down now with all this hullabaloo going on. He would have to run for office. But once Judge Cavanaugh and his bunch were where they belonged and folks once again started acting like they had some sense, he would quit, leave Gradyville, and turn the sheriff's job over to Clay.

As she often did, Laurel Remick arrived in his thoughts. She was the only person in town, besides Doc Evans, who knew about his illness, though he suspected that the young woman had confided the information to Reverend Stubby and Clay, both of whom had been acting a bit differently around him lately. He couldn't blame Laurel for letting the cat out of the bag. But he didn't want her to see him sick and weak. After all, the woman was a month or so away from marrying Clay Adams. She should be reveling in the joy of being a young bride, not standing beside his deathbed.

The coffee taken care of, Matheson sat down at his desk and tried to tend to some paperwork, but his thoughts were elsewhere. He wondered what Clay Adams would do if Clint Smith were elected sheriff. One thing was certain: Smith wouldn't keep Clay as a deputy. He'd probably give the job to one of the two toughs who were with him at the church yesterday. Matheson had to concede that the toughs were on their best behavior and probably would be for the rest of the week, spending their time in bars buying drinks and telling everyone what a swell sheriff Clint Smith would make.

The door burst open, and Adams stomped inside, back from the early-morning round. "Beau wants to see you over at the newspaper office."

"What about?"

"Better ask him."

"What's eating you?"

"Howard Lowry." Adams placed his rifle in the rack on the office wall. "When I went by the stage depot this morning, Lowry shouted out that after next Monday, I'll be able to sleep in every morning. Real funny man."

"You'd better get used to it."

"Have you been outside yet?"

"Stepped out for a few minutes very early this morning, but otherwise—"

"Let me warn you, you're not going to like what you see."

The moment Matheson left the office, he understood his deputy's warning. The town seemed blanketed by flyers, all of them proclaiming in large letters: CLINT SMITH FOR SHERIFF. Matheson sighed in a resigned manner and headed for the newspaper office.

The look on Beau Kibler's face didn't make the lawman feel any better. Kibler exchanged a few words with Tobias, who was working at the press, then motioned Matheson over to a battered rolltop desk. "Boyd, the *Gradyville Gazette* is going to support you in this election. I plan to run a series of editorials in each paper running up to the election, explaining why."

For a man who was delivering good news, Kibler looked very tense and uneasy.

"Thanks, Beau. I'm obliged."

Kibler looked at the floor, then forced his gaze back to Matheson. "There's something I need to explain."

"Go ahead."

"Boyd, there's a group of folks working hard to elect your opponent."

"I know all about that. Their names are on a petition."

The newspaper man hastily nodded his head. "Yes, of course. The point is, these people want to place advertisements for Smith in the *Gradyville Gazette,* a lot of advertisements. I don't like it, Boyd, but I am going to let them do it. I know this must sound sort of crazy, but it's a matter of ethics. The *Gazette* is Gradyville's only paper. It would be wrong for me to reject advertisements for one side in an election."

Matheson was silent, a silence Beau interpreted as disapproval. "It's not the money, Boyd! In fact, I've already turned down some money from the Smith crowd. They wanted me to print up a bunch of flyers, like the ones you see all over town now. I told them no—"

"I understand, Beau." Matheson's voice was conciliatory. He seemed to be coming out of a deep thought. "They must have had those flyers done in Tucson or someplace. What I find strange is the amount of money the Smith folks are spending on the election."

Kibler tugged on his right ear. "I've thought of that. Those flyers have been made on fine paper. Add the cost of that to all the advertising they are going to do in the *Gazette,* and, mercy, you've got more money than the office of sheriff pays for six months. Ezra Johnstone gave me the copy for the ads last night after the church service. I think he wrote them with some coaching from Smith. The ads cover pretty much the same ground as that harangue he gave at the meeting."

"Do you know who is paying?"

The newspaperman's reply was immediate. "Ezra also gave me a check he signed himself."

"No surprise. Ezra's is the first name on the petition, and, of course, he's mad at me for not releasing Zack. Can't blame a man for not thinking straight when his own kids are involved. Maybe the same applies to Judge Cavanaugh, but I don't think so."

"I noticed Clint Smith sitting next to Ezra last night. I wonder when they became such good friends."

"Don't know," Matheson admitted. "But I'm sure that Howard Lowry was told in advance about the money being returned to him. Howard usually sits in the back of the church, but last night he was right up front where everyone could see him."

"Yeah, it was quite a show when Smith returned the money."

Matheson's gaze moved around the newspaper office, but he really didn't seem to be looking at anything there. "There's something going on here, Beau. Something that has to do with a lot more than who is going to be the next sheriff of Gradyville."

"I've got a similar feeling," the newspaper man replied. "Think you can find out what that something is?"

"I'd better find out before next Monday."

As Matheson walked back to the sheriff's office, he could hear footsteps approaching fast from behind. He turned and saw Cletus Browning trying to catch up with him. "Got a few minutes to spare for an old man?"

"Cletus, I've always got time for the best jehu in the Arizona Territory. There's coffee on back at the office. Why don't we do our jawing there?"

"Mighty nice of you, Sheriff." Cletus caught up to the lawman. "But I'd rather not talk in the office and all. You see, I want this to be unofficial. I've kept some thoughts to myself because, well, I'm not certain. A man shouldn't say serious bad things 'bout another man 'less he's certain. Still, there's matters you should know."

The two men began to stroll down the boardwalk together. "What's on your mind, Cletus?"

"Remember how after the robbery at the stage depot and all, you asked me if I could identify any of the crooks?"

"Yes."

"I told you no, and I wasn't lyin'. I can't put my hand on the Good Book and swear to nothin'."

"I need to see the Mellors about a few things. Mind accompanying me to the livery?" The two men walked past the sheriff's office. Matheson was concerned that being close to an "official" place might shut Cletus off. "Now, as I see it, Cletus, you can't be positive when it comes to the holdup men, but you have your suspicions."

"Yes, Sheriff, that's right. That's surely right—'bout one of them, anyways. When I got hit on the head, I fell to the floor moanin', and one of the jaspers reached down and stuffed a bandanna into my mouth. He said, 'Shut up, you old cuss,' and I thought I recognized the voice and the eyes, from some poker games. To win at poker you gotta look at a man's eyes real careful."

"Who do you think it was?"

"Like I said, I can't swear to it, Sheriff, but I surely do believe it was Joel Hogan."

"Joel Hogan? He's never been in any trouble at all. I've never known him to even get drunk."

Cletus threw up his hands. "I know. That's another reason I didn't speak up. Joel seems a good lad. Can't imagine him doin' no holdup. But I do think I recognized the voice and eyes—"

"What about the other holdup man?"

"Can't say nothin' 'bout him. Got a quick look at him and heard his voice some, but didn't recognize nothin'."

The two men reached the end of the boardwalk. Matheson pushed his hat up a bit and scratched the front of his head. "If you're right and what Clint Smith said last night is true, then Joel Hogan is dead now."

"Yeah. I was there at the meetin' last night. Sure hope that ain't so 'bout the Hogan lad."

"Thanks for speaking up, Cletus. I know it wasn't easy."

"Whatcha gonna do now, Sheriff?"

"Think I'll ride out to the Johnstone spread and ask to speak with Joel. Can't say that I'm looking forward to it. Don't reckon that Ezra is in much of a mood to do me any favors."

As he rode out of town, Matheson spotted Laurel Remick coming out of Remick's General Store. He nodded politely and touched two fingers to his hat as he rode by. Boyd laughed a bit as Laurel threw a mischievous smile at him. He had always liked that smile.

But on this day he had no idea what the mischief was about.

Chapter Sixteen

Laurel Remick walked in a determined manner toward the Silver Creek Saloon. She had been inside the establishment many times before but still felt uncomfortable entering the place. The young woman had to work at looking casual as she nodded to a few people on the boardwalk before stepping through the bat-wing doors. Perkins experienced no such anxieties as he scampered beside her.

Inside, the Silver Creek was almost empty, as it usually was at this hour in the morning. The chairs were on the table, and a man everyone called Packy was sweeping the floor. Giving Packy a steady job was one of the many acts of kindness credited to the saloon's owner, Todd Wheeler.

"Lou, I need an eye-opener, real bad." A slumping woman in a ruffled dress spoke to the bartender.

"Okay, Sal, but only one." The bartender had been

preoccupied with getting the bar ready for the first wave of customers, which would be arriving in about an hour. He hastily set a glass on the bar and poured a drink. "You need to be careful about—"

"Yeah, yeah." Sal grabbed at the glass. Her eyes were lined with red and set back in a sickly complexion.

The bartender's face suddenly exploded with cheerfulness. "Miss Remick! We sure miss seeing you around here! Guess you've come to visit with the boss."

"Yes, if—"

Lou turned toward an open door beside the bar. "Mr. Wheeler! You got a very special guest out here!" He glanced down at the dog and then added with a laugh, "Make that two special guests."

Laurel glanced at Sal, who kept her head down, staring into the liquor.

"Miss Remick!" Todd Wheeler bounded through the open door. He was a heavyset man of average height and seemingly limitless energy. "I thought we'd never see you at the Silver Creek again, after I gave the old piano to the church."

"It was very kind of you to allow me to come in here some mornings and practice."

"The pleasure was all ours, right, Lou?" The bartender nodded his head in agreement, and Todd Wheeler continued. "Why, listening to you play those hymns gave us a real touch of heaven. And, given the kind of days we have here, Lou and I need all the reminders of heaven we can get. Most of our customers remind us of the other place."

Laurel laughed politely as the two men guffawed

over what they obviously considered to be a real knee-slapper. Laughing at Todd's jokes was a skill Laurel had honed along with her ability to play the piano.

Todd Wheeler had been surprised and delighted when Laurel had asked him if she could come into the Silver Creek two mornings a week and practice on the piano. Laurel had had no other alternatives. For several years she had been receiving lessons from Margaret McLaurty, who had a piano in her home. But when Margaret died, her kin came to town and took the piano back to Tombstone with them.

"And, Mr. Wheeler, it was so nice of you to donate the old piano to the church. You've seen for yourself what a blessing—"

"Oh, that was nothing at all."

Todd's false humility skirted the truth. After Laurel finished practicing one morning, Wheeler had casually mentioned that in a few years he would need to buy a new piano for the Silver Creek. Laurel had then suggested, very gently, that perhaps he could buy the new piano right away and donate the current one to the church. The saloon owner had paused for a few moments and then declared that, by George, that's exactly what he'd do.

Laurel noticed that Sal was looking at her while returning an empty glass to the counter. Laurel smiled and nodded. Sal quickly looked away.

The bar owner had not seen the brief exchange. "Miss Remick, why don't we go to my office? We can talk there. Perkins, you can come too. You'll have a lot more smart things to say than I will."

That remark brought another round of laughter. As she accompanied Todd through the open door beside the bar and down a short corridor, Laurel could hear a conversation beginning between Sal and the bartender.

"Please, Lou, I gotta have just one more."

"Now, what did I tell you . . ."

As they stepped into his office and Todd held a chair for his guest while he told another knee-slapper, Laurel reflected on the strange land that was the West. Todd Wheeler was regarded as one of Gradyville's finest citizens, and, in many ways, the accolade was well deserved. But the man ran a saloon with an upstairs that was used for . . .

Laurel put those thoughts out of her mind as she feigned laughter over the punch line of Todd's joke. "Mr. Wheeler, how do you think up such funny stories?"

"Well, not all the stories are mine. Some of them I get from the drummers who come through town, but, yeah, I do make a lot of them up—just sort of comes natural." Wheeler walked behind his desk and slowly sat down. "Miss Remick, I'm always honored to have a lady like you visit my establishment."

Laurel noted that Todd Wheeler's attitude toward her had always been proper. There was no reason to believe that the man was not completely devoted to his wife and four kids. Still, there was a certain glow in Todd's eyes when they talked. He wanted to please her.

"Mr. Wheeler, I know you were at the service last night."

The businessman shook his head and sighed. "Yeah. The whole thing made me mad. Boyd Matheson has done a great job as sheriff of this town. He's sure been a help to me. He knows the difference between a hard case and a drunken cowboy. Not all star packers do. And as long as things don't get out of hand, he doesn't give me any problems about my girls. Matheson understands that—"

Todd Wheeler's face suddenly turned red. He turned his head and cleared his throat.

A quick change was needed here. "Mr. Wheeler, have you seen the flyers that are posted around town for Clint Smith?" Laurel laughed at herself. "That's a silly question. There's no way you could miss them."

Todd was grateful for having a new subject tossed to him. "Those things are everywhere, all right."

"And I hear that there are going to be a lot of newspaper advertisements urging people to vote for Clint Smith."

The bar owner made a low whistle. "I guess Ezra Johnstone is really opening up his wallet."

Laurel reached down, scratched Perkins' right ear for a moment, then continued. "Mr. Wheeler, I don't know if you realize it, but you are regarded as, well, a community leader in Gradyville."

"Well, thank you, Miss Remick. Sure is nice of you to say that."

"Mr. Wheeler, could you help Sheriff Matheson? I've already talked to Beau Kibler, and he will make up flyers for the sheriff and not charge for his work, but he needs someone to pay for the paper."

"Well . . ."

"And could you place some advertisements in the *Gradyville Gazette?*"

"You see, Miss Remick, it's just good business sense for bar owner to stay out of politics. Men vote all sorts of ways, but after they vote, they come in for a drink. It wouldn't be smart to take sides in an election. Why make some of your customers mad at you?"

"No one would be mad at you, Mr. Wheeler. Why, they'd respect you even more—a leader who put his own name on a newspaper advertisement for Sheriff Matheson and urged others to follow his example, a man who has the courage to really live out his convictions!"

"Well . . ."

"The West needs men like you. Men who will stand up for what's right."

Todd Wheeler went silent for a moment, then slammed a fist onto his desk. "By George, that's exactly what I'll do! I'll go see Beau Kibler this morning. The other side has a head start on us but, by George, we'll give them a race!"

"Oh, thank you, Mr. Wheeler. You really are a wonderful man!"

Todd smiled broadly and may have blushed a bit as he looked down. Laurel used the moment to shake an index finger twice in front of Perkins' face. The dog responded to the signal by barking two times.

"You see? Even Perkins thinks you're wonderful!" Laurel reached down and gave the dog a hug, his reward for successfully executing the trick.

There were several more minutes of laughter and excited talk about the election. As she left Todd Wheeler's office and passed the bar, Laurel noticed that Sal was no longer there. Lou wished her a good day. Packy was taking the chairs off the tables.

Walking briskly back to Remick's General Store, Laurel wondered a bit about what she had just done. Somewhere around the age of thirteen, Laurel had begun to notice that with a pleasant smile and a compliment she could get men to do what she wanted them to do. The young woman had always been cautious not to over-use this power. But she knew that Boyd Matheson would never ask anyone to spend serious money to help re-elect him as sheriff. Surely it was not wrong for her to get Todd Wheeler to organize and finance a campaign for a sheriff that he himself admired.

Still, Laurel couldn't be completely sure. As she neared the general store, the young woman glanced down at Perkins. "Maybe I should talk with Reverend Steuben about this." Perkins looked up at her, interested, but he didn't bark.

"Yes," she said to the canine, "I might talk to the pastor about the whole matter. But I don't think I'll do it until *after* the election."

Chapter Seventeen

As he rode toward the Johnstone ranch house, Matheson saw a cowhand named Wade walking toward the house from the corral. Wade also spotted the lawman; shock visibly coursed through his body, and his right hand hovered over his gun. Matheson sighed deeply. Wade was a hothead who drank too much every Saturday night. "At least this morning, the man is probably sober," Boyd said to his horse.

Matheson dismounted in front of the ranch house and tied his roan to the hitch rail. He pretended not to see Wade.

"Whadda you want?"

Matheson turned around casually and smiled. "Good morning, Wade."

"I said, whadd'ya want?"

"Oh, I just need to talk with Ezra some—nothing to get riled about." The lawman stepped around the rail and was almost on the porch when Wade grabbed him by one shoulder and turned him around.

"Maybe the boss don't want to talk to you."

"Ezra can speak for himself. Back off, Wade. No need to cause trouble."

"I'm orderin' you to leave!" Wade went for his gun. Matheson delivered a hard punch to the bridge of the man's nose. Wade stumbled backward and fell over the hitch rail, his gun spinning into the air and hitting the ground moments after its owner.

The lawman stepped quickly around the hitch rail and picked up the gun. "I'll just hold on to this until I leave. Why don't you get back to work, and we'll forget—"

Wade put a hand to his nose, then stared at the red blotch that covered his fingers. "I'll show you!"

He scrambled to his feet and charged Matheson. The sheriff started to hit Wade with his own pistol but thought better of it and delivered a hard left against the cowhand's cheekbone. Wade flopped back to the ground.

"Surprised you, huh?" Matheson said good-naturedly. "I can use my left hand as well as my right. There's a big word for it, *ambidextrous*."

"I'll show you," Wade repeated, but this time he got to his feet much more slowly.

"Wade!" a female voice shouted from the porch.

"Hello, Miss Esther." Matheson touched two fingers to his hat.

"Good morning, Sheriff. Wade, what are you doing?"

"This lawdog came onto our property with no permission." The cowhand was on his feet but more than a bit unsteady.

"Sheriff Matheson doesn't need permission. He's always welcome here."

"Your pa would say different."

Esther's face contorted for a moment. Wade's statement was true, and it hurt her to admit it. "Go to the well and throw some water onto your wounds. My father should be back soon. I'll see that the sheriff is taken care of until then."

"All right." Wade walked sullenly toward the well. He didn't like taking instructions from a girl of fourteen.

Esther stepped off the porch and smiled at the lawman. "I'm sorry, Sheriff Matheson."

"There's nothing for you to be sorry about, Miss Esther. Wade is just feeling a bit ornery this morning. I get that way sometimes myself." He handed her the six-shooter. "Could you return that to Wade? No need to hurry about it."

"Of course, Sheriff Matheson." A broad smiled spread over Esther's face as she took the weapon. She was obviously pleased that Matheson had given her the responsibility.

Hoofbeats sounded as Ezra Johnstone rode to the hitch rail and quickly dismounted. He glanced at Wade, who was staggering toward the well.

"Haven't you caused us enough grief, Sheriff?" Ezra tossed his horse's reins around the rail and approached the lawman. "Why are you here making trouble, and who is in town guarding my son?"

"Pa, Wade was the one who made trouble—"

"Get inside the house, right now. You have work to do."

Esther Johnstone obeyed her father but didn't try to hide her anguish. Tears left random lines on her cheeks as she returned to the house, slamming the door behind her.

For a moment a strange look overwhelmed Ezra Johnstone's face, a look of regret and disgust for the man he was becoming. But that look quickly vanished, replaced with a mask of hostility.

"You are not welcome here, Sheriff."

"I won't stay long, Mr. Johnstone." Matheson turned his head momentarily as two cowhands rode toward the corral. "But I need to talk with you a moment. Inside would be better. A man's reputation is at stake here."

Without speaking, Ezra walked across the porch and into his house, motioning for Matheson to follow him. As he walked through the doorway, Matheson remembered the last time he had been at the Johnstone ranch, the day he and Clay had been tracking the bank robbers. Ezra had treated the two lawmen as if they were family. That seemed a long time ago.

The two men stepped into the living room. Ezra turned and faced Matheson. "Make it quick. I have a lot to do."

"I'm here about one of your ranch hands, Joel Hogan."

"He's not here anymore."

"Did you fire him?'

"No, he just disappeared one day. Didn't show when it was time for work."

"When was that?"

"I can't remember, a few days back."

"One of your own men just disappeared. Didn't you look into it, Mr. Johnstone?"

"Cowhands are born with itchy feet. They take off all the time."

"Not without getting the pay that was due them, and Joel Hogan was a very levelheaded young man. Not the kind to just run off."

"I'm running a ranch here, Sheriff! I got no time to be a mother hen."

"Did another hand just up and disappear at the same time?"

"No!" Ezra closed his eyes for a moment, shook his head, and then continued. "Well, maybe."

"What was the name of the other hand?"

"I can't remember. Look, I've wasted enough time jawing with you."

"I need to talk with Ned Myers. Where would he be right now?"

"My foreman could be anywhere. Who knows? Maybe he's gone into town for something."

"I'll find him. Thanks for your time."

Matheson was at the front door when the ranch owner shouted at him, "What are you going to bother Ned Myers about?"

The lawman opened the door and turned to face the rancher. "I'm hoping Ned's memory is a bit better than yours. Good day, Mr. Johnstone."

As he stepped onto the front porch, Matheson thought he heard the sound of light footsteps running along the side of the ranch house. When he got to his roan, he found a note tied to the horn of the saddle with a piece of string. He read the neat handwriting, then patted his horse and spoke softly. "Maybe I don't need to see Ned Myers after all."

Chapter Eighteen

Russ Cavanaugh peered through the bars at the man in the cell next to his. "You're nothing but a little kid, Zack."

Zack Johnstone lowered the book he was reading and smirked at his neighbor. "Not everyone can be smart and successful like you, Russ."

"Ya wake up every morning with the sun."

"Best time of the day."

"Then read the Good Book and pray."

"True, but how'd you know, Russ? You're always sawing logs."

"Ya woke me up once. Besides, I know what kind ya are. After Bible reading, ya read that other thing."

Zack held up the book. "Its called *Pilgrim's Progress* by a man named John Bunyan. The reverend loaned it to me. The story is about a man who makes some bad mistakes but still gets his life in order. I've made some really dumb mistakes. Now I gotta get busy on the other part."

Cavanugh laughed in a derisive manner. "I was never one to put much stock in fairy tales."

Zack looked carefully at his childhood friend. Russ Cavanaugh's eyes were wild, but with what? Anger? Insanity, maybe? Several days in jail had given him a ragged appearance, making the Buffalo Bill hair and beard look laughable.

Johnstone lay the book down and sat up on the cot where he had been reading. "For a man who doesn't care for fairy tales, you were sure lapping up what Clint Smith said an hour or so back."

"What are ya talking about?"

"You know what I mean." Zack stood up and took a few steps toward his neighbor. They were now less than two feet apart. "Smith was here telling you about how he'll see to it that the whole town knows the truth about you killing the bank robbers and returning the money, all about how the mean sheriff and his deputy blamed you for the holdup just because you're Judge Cavanaugh's son. Why, they even buried the robbers in unmarked graves to hide their deception. Even a fool like me could tell what he was really doing. He was feeding you the lies so you won't contradict him when anyone asks what happened. Well, it's not going to work, Russ."

"And just why not?"

"Are you forgetting what you really did after holding up the bank? I know the truth, and my days of lying for you are over." Zack turned away and returned to his book.

Russ Cavanaugh also turned away. He had confirmed his suspicions. Zack Johnstone would have to be killed.

"Yeah, boys, the way I see it, Sheriff Matheson is sorta like a mule." Clint Smith put down his glass. It was only his second drink. But the four men sitting with him at a table in the Roman Holiday Saloon were far past that point. "He kicks real good, but he's not fussy enough about who he kicks. Well, when I become sheriff, I'll see to it that the people who deserve it get kicked, and hard-working men like yourselves are left alone."

All four men broke into laughter and cheers. Clint smiled and tossed a bill onto the table. "Enjoy another bottle on me. See you later."

The gunfighter kept a smile on his face as he strolled out of the Roman Holiday and nodded to a few passersby. So far, politics seemed like a pretty easy game. No matter where you went, there was always an abundance of fools and riffraff; just get them all lined up on your side, and you had a majority.

Clint Smith strolled toward the sheriff's office. He wondered why Russ Cavanaugh had been so insistent that he come by again in a couple of hours. Of course, there was no telling what was going on in the loco mind of that one. No wonder his daddy planned to kill him once they got him out of jail.

Clay Adams looked up from his desk and gave the visitor a harsh stare. "Back again, Smith?"

"Just want to jaw with Russ for a few minutes."

Adams stood up and approached the visitor. "You'll have—"

"I know, Deputy." Smith took off his gun belt and handed it to the lawman. He then emptied the contents of his pockets onto the desk. "You're not going to make me take off my boots again, are you?"

"Yes."

The gunman sat down on a chair in front of the desk, took off his boots, and stood up. Adams checked the boots, then quickly patted Smith from his ankles to his shoulders.

"Okay, put your boots back on, and go talk to Cavanaugh. I've heard some reports about you, Smith. You're sure having an interesting morning, jawing with a killer and buying drinks for barflies."

The gunman walked toward the jail area without speaking. Adams had managed to take the grin off Smith's face; that made the deputy feel good.

Then the lawman looked at the scattering of items on his desk. There among the cigarette makings was a money clip. Adams' eyes widened as he picked it up and counted the bills. Clint Smith had plenty of money to spend on buying drinks in order to buy votes, and there were plenty of barflies in Gradyville.

The deputy no longer felt good.

Russ Cavanaugh held a finger to his lips and motioned Smith to come near his cell. "That Zack Johnstone is like clockwork." He pointed to the next cell. "Always naps about this time, an hour or so before eating lunch."

"You brought me here just to tell me that?" Smith's

voice wasn't a whisper. Zack stirred a bit but didn't wake up.

"Keep it down." Russ motioned downward with his hand, keeping his voice very low. "Johnstone knows everything about what happened. I mean, really happened. Ya need ta take care of it."

"You're telling me to kill him."

"That's exactly what I'm doing."

"How do you expect me to kill a man who is in jail?"

"That's your problem. The judge is paying ya good money. Maybe it's time ya started earning it."

"Well, I got rid of Jarrett easy enough while he was in the doctor's office, but this will be a bit tougher."

"You get rid of Zack. And stop by here at this time every day. I want reports on what's going on. After I'm outta here, I'm going to tell the judge what kind of job ya did."

Smith stopped whispering. "Russ, I'll sure be happy when the day comes that you're no longer in this place." He smiled broadly and returned to the office area to retrieve his stuff. He heard the deputy say something about his money but paid it no heed.

Smith walked toward the livery and his horse. The judge had told him to stay away from the hideout until after the election, but that just wasn't possible. He was sure the judge would understand.

Still, as he mounted up, Clint Smith felt a needle of fear press into him.

Chapter Nineteen

Matheson watched as the rider drew closer. He hoped something would come of this. He had been waiting longer than he had expected.

"Hello, Sheriff Matheson." The girl spoke as she dismounted. "After I wrote the note, I got worried, afraid you might not know where moon rock was."

Matheson looked to the other side of the trail, where there was a hill big enough that some called it a mountain. At the very top perched a large stone shaped like a full moon. "I guess most everyone in town knows about moon rock, Miss Esther."

"Guess so." The girl's face became wistful. "I wanted to meet you here not only because it's out of the way but this is where Tommy and I used to meet. Something terrible has happened to Tommy, Sheriff."

Matheson didn't know who Tommy was, but the girl

had a lot inside her that needed to be turned loose. He said nothing.

"That Tommy Skerrit is really something. Do you know what he once told me?"

"No, Miss Esther."

The girl looked up at the unique stone. "He said that after we got married and had our own ranch, he'd climb to the top of that hill and bring down moon rock for me. He'd put it right beside the barn, and every time I looked at it, I'd be reminded of how much he loved me."

Esther's head moved downward, and she was quiet, mourning a vanished dream. When the girl spoke again, the wistfulness was gone from her face. "Things are bad at the ranch, Sheriff, real bad, and it's affecting everyone like some bad disease. You saw how Wade acted. I'm the only one who will admit that something's wrong."

"Tell me about it as best you can, Miss Esther."

"Father has just—he's gone crazy. He's always cared about the men who worked for him. Now he doesn't seem to care about Tommy. No, it's worse than that. Father knows something bad has happened, and he just wants to pretend that it's not so. Wants everybody to pretend."

"Are they?"

The girl nodded. "Ned Myers is busy teaching Jim how to run the ranch. And he's learning good. My brother has really grown up since our mother died. But Ned and Jim are both ignoring the changes in Father— or trying hard to. They're hoping it will all pass, and the real Ezra Johnstone will come back. That's not going to happen, Sheriff. The man I've always known as my father—that man is gone forever."

"Can you remember when these changes in Ezra got started?"

"When Clint Smith arrived." She laughed bitterly. "The Arizona Ranger who was going to help Zack."

"Smith told your father that he was an Arizona Ranger?"

Esther lowered her voice slightly. "I'm not supposed to know about that. Father sent Jim and me away so he could have a private conversation with Mr. Smith. But I listened from the kitchen. I could hear Mr. Smith say that he was an Arizona Ranger. Later on he told father that sometimes Rangers had to break the law."

"What else did you hear?"

"Not much, but after supper I met Tommy right here. He was late, but when he arrived, he was more excited than a bird after a worm. Tommy told me that something very special was going to happen the next day. That my father was really going to admire him—wouldn't think of him as some green kid who wasn't worthy of his daughter. Everything was going to be wonderful. . . ."

The girl suddenly stopped and pulled a handkerchief from her pocket. She dabbed her eyes for a moment. "I'm sorry."

"Don't worry, Miss Esther, just take your time."

She returned the handkerchief to her pocket. "Guess I really don't have much more to say. Tommy wouldn't tell me what it was about—said that would spoil everything."

"Think carefully, Miss Esther. Did Tommy say what time of day this special thing was going to happen?"

Esther was quiet for a moment. "Yes, he said it would

happen in the morning. Sunday morning. I'm sure of that."

"Was anybody else going to be helping him, or was he doing it by himself?"

"Oh!" Esther's hands flew up, fingers spread. "I forgot to tell you! Joel Hogan! Joel is a friend of Tommy's—more of a big brother, really. Joel Hogan and Tommy were both in on it. In fact, Joel was sort of the leader. Somebody asked Joel to do something and get one person to help him. He got Tommy."

"Do you have any idea who that somebody who talked to Joel was?"

"No."

"When Tommy told you about this special thing he was involved with, was he, well, a bit edgy? Did he say anything that might make you think that he and Joel were going to do something that was against the law?"

The girl shook her head vigorously. "No, Sheriff. That's impossible. I know Tommy. When he's doing wrong, he gets as nervous as a cat under a rocking chair. If he was about to break the law, I would have known it. Tommy is good at a lot of things, but he's one terrible liar."

There was another short period of silence, until Esther spoke in a near whisper. "Sheriff, is there any chance that you may find my Tommy and bring him back to me?" A look of hope flickered in her eyes.

Matheson watched it die as he shook his head. "I wouldn't count on that, Miss Esther."

Esther cringed as if absorbing an assault. "Thank you for coming here, Sheriff Matheson. I hope I've been of some help." The young woman started to look upward, then hastily averted her eyes from moon rock. She again thanked the lawman for meeting with her, then mounted her horse and rode off.

Matheson stood and watched her slowly disappear. At first he comforted himself with the usual thoughts. Esther was very young. There would be more young men courting her. She'd find someone, settle down, and have a good life.

Boyd Matheson angrily kicked the ground in front of him. No. That wasn't good enough. Two young men had been killed after robbing the stage depot. And, somehow, they had been convinced that the robbery was an act of good. The lawman was convinced that Joel Hogan and Tommy Skerrit had paid a terrible price for being young and naive.

And Esther Johnstone would never really be young again. Matheson patted his roan. "I may not be sheriff after next Monday, but I'll see to it that Clint Smith and the judge get everything they deserve."

Chapter Twenty

The gunman knocked quietly on the door of the cabin.

"Who is it?"

"It's Clint, Your Honor."

The silence that followed made Smith jittery. He glanced at the two men who sat under a nearby tree playing cards. The rest of the outfit was in town, buying drinks and urging men to vote for Clint Smith. The two remaining men looked at Smith curiously. He wasn't supposed to be here. The gunman couldn't be sure, but he thought he saw a glint of amusement in the eyes of both men. The judge was going to be mad. Their long, hot afternoon might be broken up by a bit of entertainment at the expense of Clint Smith.

"Come in."

The gunman almost stumbled into the cabin where Judge Cavanaugh, as usual, was sitting at a table, engrossed in some papers. "Your Honor, I'm sorry to—"

The judge studiously ignored Clint. He dipped his pen into a bottle of ink and continued to write, never even shifting his gaze to the gunman.

Once again Clint wondered what those papers were all about. His boss seemed to constantly have his head bent over those things.

When Judge Cavanaugh glanced up from his work, there was a wide smile on his face, but his eyes were distant. "Clint, we agreed that you were not to come here until after the election. I assume that you have a good reason for disobeying my order. You must be bringing very good news for me. You persuaded the people of Gradyville to release Russ. Yes, that must be it."

"No, no, Your Honor, that's not—"

"Then what is it?!"

"You see, sir, elections can be sort of tricky. I've had to say some things I hadn't planned on."

"Like . . ."

"Well, like you and me talked about earlier, I told folks that you weren't responsible for the attack on the prayer meeting. That it was all newspaper lies to make you look bad. I said that Russ had been framed by Matheson and that other lawdog. And then . . ."

"Speak up! And then what?" Cavanaugh shouted.

"I told them that you'd make a personal appearance sometime during the election."

Cavanaugh's body trembled with anger. He made a fist and almost pounded it against the table but realized that the table was too rickety to withstand the force. The judge lurched from his chair and stormed out of the cabin.

Even in his nervous state, Clint Smith couldn't pass up a rare opportunity. He glanced down at the judge's papers and gasped out loud at what he read.

The wealthy railroad owner pointed at the stacks of money on his desk. "So, Judge Cavanaugh, you won't accept my generous bribe."

"I want no part of your filthy lucre," the judge said.

"Have it your way." The rich man snapped his fingers. Four gunmen stepped into the room.

Judge Cavanaugh's hands hovered over the two pearl-handled revolvers that were strapped to his waist. "Any time you're ready, gentlemen."

Bullets whizzed across the room. The rich man ducked under his desk. When he lifted his head up, only one man was still standing. Judge Cavanaugh now held a smoking revolver in each hand. "Your days of stepping on poor, hardworking citizens are over, rich man. . . ."

Clint Smith hastily stepped away from the table and tried to suppress his astonishment. Judge Lewis Rutherford Cavanaugh spent most of his days writing dime novels about himself! Smith wondered if all that talk Cavanaugh gave him about becoming governor was just another fantasy concocted by a man who spent his days writing yarns that told the world he was a glorious hero.

Smith listened carefully and glanced out the back window. His boss was walking around the cabin, muttering to himself and walking toward the two henchmen stationed outside. Was the judge about to order the two gunmen to fire on Clint Smith? No. By stretching his neck a bit, Clint could see that Cavanaugh was having one of his occasional friendly chats with the paid help. Even Judge Lewis Rutherford Cavanaugh knew that he couldn't stay aloof from his men at all times.

Clint Smith thought about the strange man who was his boss as he walked back to the table. Judge Cavanaugh was not a fool; writing dime novels was a clever way the judge had of convincing people that he was a Robin Hood. Someday, Lewis Rutherford Cavanaugh would be governor, and Clint Smith would be his right hand.

Smith hastily lifted the manuscript from the table and glanced at the title page: *Judge Cavanaugh v. The Railroad Barons* by Graham Ellison. With an inaudible sigh of relief, he set the manuscript back down. His boss had the good sense not to write about himself using his own name. A smart idea, really, and who would ever know?

An explosion of laughter interrupted Smith's thinking. A smiling Judge Cavanaugh reentered the cabin. "A brilliant idea, Clint! The story of this escapade will spread across the West—across the nation! The reputation of Judge Cavanaugh will be solidified forever. I'll coast into the position of mayor of Tucson, and—"

The judge stopped and bent over his desk. For a moment, Smith feared, irrationally, that his boss might notice that his papers had been read. But, no, the judge hastily scribbled something and handed it to his top henchman.

"There are the names and addresses of two reporters who, uh, can be depended on to write the truth about me. One is with the *Standard* in Tucson. The other works for the *Nugget* in Tombstone. Wire them to come to Gradyville—we will pay their expenses. It'll be worth it, as long as they are there when I make an appearance. When do you plan to carry this scheme out?"

"Saturday night."

"Good! That's when we'll have the biggest crowd." A slight edge returned to the judge's voice. "I'm certain that you have a plan to carry all this out in a manner that will make it impossible for the law to arrest me."

"Of course." Smith sounded confident, even cheerful. "But first I'm going to set the stage. Get folks in town really hating those lawdogs."

"How do you propose to do that?"

The gunman looked nervous again; he had lots of vague ideas in his head but nothing definite. "I'm gonna try a lot of things, Your Honor. And I bet every one of them works."

"They'd better." Cavanaugh's smile remained, but a ferocious glare flamed in his eyes, and, for a moment, Clint Smith wondered if he was looking into the face of the devil.

Chapter Twenty-One

Orin Mellor set his glass back down on the bar. "Sure I can't pay you none, Mr. Wheeler?"

"You sure can, Orin. Give that horse of mine a free bag of oats."

Todd Wheeler chortled along with Orin and Lou, the bartender. Orin had stopped at the Silver Creek Saloon for a bit of refreshment before continuing his round.

The saloon owner made a fist and tapped Orin on the shoulder. "It's a fine thing you and your pa do, serving as unpaid deputies. Must be harder than ever right now. Are you still able to keep up the livery okay?"

"Oh, sure. Pa and me mostly don't do deputy work at the same time. One of us is usually with the nags. Of course, it ain't just the two of us. My older boys can help now."

"The Mellors operate a fine livery." Lou topped off Orin's glass. "Everyone says so."

"Thanks, but Mellor's Livery is proof that luck is one very strange lady."

"What do you mean?" Wheeler asked.

"If Pa and me hadn't got hurt when the mine blowed up, we'd never have started the livery, and we make a lot more money tending to nags then we did under the ground."

"How's it coming along?" Lou pointed at Orin's right leg.

"I'll always be a gimp, but that don't make no nevermind. Still get around fine. My dancing days are over, but then, I never could keep up on the dance floor nohow."

The men guffawed. Orin finished his drink, thanked Todd for the free refreshment, picked up the double-barrel that was propped against the bar, and strode out of the saloon. He walked north toward the church, planning to turn around there and make his way back by another route to the sheriff's office.

Orin heard sounds of harsh, raucous laughter. The kind of laughter that meant trouble. He picked up his stride and saw three men, two on one side of the street and one on the other, ripping down flyers. Flyers that read: REELECT BOYD MATHESON AS SHERIFF.

No need for the shotgun, not yet, Orin yanked a .44 from its holster and fired into the air.

"What's botherin' you, stable boy?" the man working the side of the street by himself shouted.

"Leave them flyers alone." Orin holstered the .44.

"You should be thankin' us, stable boy," the same owlhoot said. "George, Harry, and me is just clearing away some trash."

"I knows for a fact that a lot of people worked hard on them flyers." Orin tried to keep careful track of the three men who were now approaching him. "Beau Kibler was working most of the night on the printing."

"Well, if he's so all-fired excited 'bout reelecting the sheriff, he can just stay up again tonight and do it all over." The same man spoke again; he was obviously the leader of the threesome.

The leader and George were now standing in front of Orin. One of the oldest tricks in the book, Orin thought to himself. Both the leader and George began babbling at the deputy, trying to hold his attention.

Orin could hear steps advancing on him from behind. He swung around and landed both barrels of his shotgun on the side of Harry's skull. Harry dropped to the ground, falling, ironically, on the pistol that he had intended to use on Orin's head.

Still gripping the shotgun in both hands, Orin rammed the butt into George's midriff. George had charged at Orin, by instinct probably—the owlhoot didn't seem to have any plan in mind. But the entire matter was now moot. George lay doubled up on the ground, groaning along with Harry.

The leader held up both hands in a stop gesture. "Hey, Deputy, don't go gettin' all excited. The boys just got a little carried away."

"You said you was interested in getting rid of trash. Well, get these two skunks out of here. And from now on, don't touch any flyers."

From the ground, Harry managed to stop groaning and to put together a sentence. "I need a doc."

"Okay, okay," the one standing thug snapped.

Orin stood and watched silently as the leader got Harry and George back onto their feet and began to walk them toward Doc Evans' place. "Politics is one crazy business," he said to himself, then continued his round.

Chapter Twenty-Two

The day after Orin's run-in with Smith's henchmen, the following story appeared in the *Gradyville Gazette,* written by Beau Kibler.

Smith Campaign Workers Accuse Deputy of Violent Interference

Darby Hackett, a volunteer for the campaign to elect Clint Smith sheriff, has claimed that he and two other volunteers were assaulted by a sheriff's deputy while putting up handbills for Smith.

"George, Harry, and me was putting up signs for Clint Smith when this deputy attacks us. He smashes Harry on the head with a shotgun and rams that same double-barrel into George's stomach. Then

he tells us that we better not put up no more signs or he'll blow us into Mexico."

The deputy involved in the incident was Orin Mellor. Orin runs Mellor's Livery with his father, Hank. Both men serve as volunteer deputies for Sheriff Boyd Matheson. Sheriff Matheson is running against Smith to keep his office.

Orin Mellor gives a much different account of what happened. "They weren't putting up nothing. They was tearing down signs for Boyd Matheson. I told them to stop. Then they tried an old trick. Two of them talks real fast to me while the third sneaks up from behind to hit me. I didn't fall for it. I hit the one from behind with my double-barrel, then stuck the gun into the stomach of another one who came at me. After that, they left for the doc. Nothing more to it. I didn't say a thing about Mexico."

Herbert and Sarah Carnes, who were walking to the bank at the time, saw Orin hit a man who was approaching him from behind. Herbert has stated that the man was carrying a revolver and seemed ready to attack the deputy. Sarah is uncertain. "I can't say that I saw a gun. The man may have been going up to Orin to tap him on the shoulder."

Ollie Jones claims to have witnessed the entire incident. Herbert and Sarah state that they didn't see him there. Ollie backs up the version of the story

*given by Darby Hackett. Ollie Jones spends his days
at the Roman Holiday Saloon. Ken Bradford, a bartender at the saloon, told this reporter that Ollie
seems to have more money to buy drinks of late.*

*Clint Smith claims that Sheriff Matheson is trying
to sabotage his campaign. "Hank and Orin Mellor
are two hard cases Matheson uses for his own pur-
poses. Hank was supposed to guard Walter Jarrett.
But Jarrett gets killed while Hank Mellor's on guard.
Then Orin Mellor attacks my campaign workers. I
say that is mighty interesting."*

*Boyd Matheson has stated that he accepts Orin
Mellor's account of the incident. "Both Orin and
Hank are fine men who have proven their honesty
many times. They will remain volunteer deputies.
That's that."*

Boyd Matheson had been standing behind his desk
as he read the story. He casually tossed the paper down
and smiled at the only other man in the office who was
nervously pacing about. "You did a good job. Though,
I'll have to admit, the main thing I'm interested in reading in the *Gazette* is the latest installment of *A Tale of
Two Cities*. You're good, Beau, but you're no Charlie
Dickens."

Matheson's joke did nothing for Kibler's bad mood.
"Boyd, I'm sorry. But the accusations those stupid thugs
made against you, well, they're news. I had to report it."

"Sure, you're just doing—"

"But I know it's all lies!" Beau threw both arms toward the ceiling. "Judge Cavanaugh made his threats against this town through me. I sure didn't make that up. But the threats didn't work, so now the judge is trying a new tactic with Clint Smith as his mouthpiece. Or maybe the tail is wagging the dog—who knows? But Cavanaugh and Smith are the villains of this piece, not you and the Mellors. Why—"

"Beau, you wrote about what the judge did to you in the *Gazette.*"

"Yeah, but how many people remember that? Folks are like tumbleweeds in a windstorm. Their minds go every which way, never settling anywhere."

"That's not true of all folks, Beau."

"Hope you're right." Beau Kibler paused; an embarrassed look fell over his face. "Boyd, do you think of being a lawman as, well, something of a calling?"

"A calling?"

"Yes, you know, like Reverend Stubby has a calling to preach."

Matheson smiled in a kindly manner but didn't laugh. Beau was trying to be very serious and having some problems doing it. The sheriff didn't want to further his discomfort. "Well, yes, since you've put it that way, I do think that being a lawman is a calling. Have even said so on occasion."

"I feel the same way about being a newspaperman." Kibler's gaze skedaddled about the office. "But being a good newspaperman meant I had to print a bunch of crazy lies some morons spouted." Beau once again began to pace about the office. "I want to inform people, make them better citizens, but sometimes the job is just not what it's supposed to be."

"I know exactly how you feel, Beau."

"What do you mean?"

"A lawman's duty is to protect civilization."

That response caused the journalist to immediately stop his pacing. He gave Matheson a questioning stare. "Yes, but what's your point?"

"Sometimes civilization is just not what it's supposed to be."

Chapter Twenty-Three

Judge Cavanaugh finished reading the newspaper article for a second time, then placed the *Gradyville Gazette* on the rickety table that he referred to as his desk. "Excellent, Clint, excellent."

"When Darby told me what happened, I saw a way to get something good out of it. I made up the story and had Darby take it to the newspaperman."

"And there will be plenty of fools who will believe it. You put another dent into Boyd Matheson's armor. You have the makings of a good politician, Clint."

"Thanks, Judge. Now, if you don't mind, I'd like you to step outside for a moment and see what we got planned for this Saturday night."

Cavanaugh stood up, but a look of irritation settled over his face. The judge was the one who decided when he would mix with the paid underlings.

Clint Smith caught his boss' displeasure. "You're going to be surprised by what's out there, Your Honor, but I know you're going to like it."

The judge's grouchiness diminished but did not vanish as the two men stepped outside of the cabin. There was a large box-shaped wagon there painted white with the words *Dr. Smiley's Medicine Show* in garish red on both sides of the wagon.

"You don't expect me to lower—"

"Of course not, Judge. I'm going to ride this wagon into Gradyville this Saturday night. Hired a banjo player from the Roman Holiday to sit beside me and play a few tunes as I ride in. When the crowd gathers round, I'll make some jokes. The law will gather at the wagon. They'll think you're inside the thing, getting ready to make an appearance."

Cavanaugh fiddled nervously with his pipe. "Go on."

Clint motioned toward one of the henchmen, who approached leading a white horse. "Your Honor, you know Darby—he's the one who found us the medicine wagon and the white horse. It was my idea, of course. I even told Darby where to look—"

"Why do we need the white horse?" Cavanaugh's nervousness seemed to increase.

"Why, that's for you, Judge," Smith quickly responded. "I'll have the wagon in the center of town. Then you ride in from the south on a white horse, firing a gun just like—" Clint stopped. He had almost said, *"just like in those dime novels you write."* He settled for, ". . . just like the Robin Hood of Arizona. You shout at all the good folks to vote for me, then ride off."

"But, like you said, the law will be there—"

"Yeah, but I don't think any of them will take after you."

"How can you be so sure?"

"While you and me is making all that commotion, Darby is going to pay a little visit to the sheriff's office. He'll free Russ and kill Zack Johnstone and whoever is acting as the deputy. Of course, he'll wait until he sees you riding out of town before he fires his gun. Shots coming from the sheriff's office. The lawdogs will have their hands full. They won't have time to come after you. But, just in case—" Clint made a sweeping gesture that took in the rest of the gang. "We'll have plenty of men there to slow them down."

Judge Cavanaugh still looked skeptical. "Getting Russ out of jail won't be easy."

"Might be easier than you think." Clint Smith smiled broadly. "Ezra Johnstone is going to help us. The official story for the newspaper will be that Ezra tried to break his son out of jail, and, in the process, the deputy killed Zack and stopped a bullet himself. Meanwhile, Russ managed to escape."

"Of course, you'll have to kill the old man too."

"Yeah, you're right, of course."

Chapter Twenty-Four

Laurel Remick stooped down and petted her small brown dog. "I know this will be fun for you, but your mistress sometimes acts in a way that ladies are not supposed to act."

The dog barked and wagged his tail. Laurel and Perkins were outside Remick's General Store. The dog sensed that they were going on a walk of some kind and was eager to get started.

"You're right. If I am going to make a fool of myself, there is no sense in delaying it." Laurel carefully wrapped a blanket around an object, tucked it under her right arm, and walked at a fast clip toward the sheriff's office. She was relieved that Clay Adams did not see her approach. He was in the office, and, if he spotted her, would probably step out and inquire as to what she was up to.

Laurel loved Clay deeply and wouldn't do anything

to hurt him. But there was this one special thing she needed to do before she became his bride.

The young woman walked up the stairs that sided the office and led to Boyd Matheson's private living quarters. Laurel did not look around her. All of those visits to the Silver Creek Saloon to practice on the piano had honed the skill of looking purposeful and free of concern while engaging in what some folks would regard as scandalous behavior.

She knocked lightly on the door. Laurel knew Matheson's schedule well. He was inside, eating his lunch and reading.

Matheson looked surprised when he opened the door. Ladies did not appear unescorted at a gentleman's home. At least, they were not supposed to. But Laurel saw a lot more in Boyd Matheson's eyes than just surprise.

"Uh, hello, Miss Remick."

"Good afternoon, Mr. Matheson." Laurel gave him that mischievous smile she knew he couldn't resist.

Matheson looked to the sky for a moment, as if hoping something would be written there that would tell him what to do next. Seeing nothing of the kind, he proceeded on his own. "Uh, won't you come in?"

"Yes, thank you." Laurel stepped inside. Perkins followed. Matheson closed the door.

"I hope I haven't interrupted your reading." Laurel nodded at a small desk, where there was a plate with nothing left of the sheriff's lunch except a few crumbs. On the right side of the plate was a cup of coffee, and on the left was a copy of *Roughing It*.

"I was about finished anyway. Need to get back to work soon."

"Mark Twain is one of my favorite writers," Laurel said. "I've read *Roughing It* twice."

Boyd Matheson smiled and relaxed a bit. "Twain can sure make you laugh. I'm mighty grateful that the reverend lent me that book. There hasn't been much to laugh about around here lately."

Laurel wanted to keep up the relaxed atmosphere. "Reverend Steuben is working to start a library in Gradyville. Meanwhile, he's something of a one-man library all by himself."

Boyd Matheson smiled broadly. "Guess he is, at that."

The young woman paused, then changed the subject. "I've been going through a lot of my things, lately, deciding what I should take with me to the house once Clay and I are married."

"It's a fine house. I know you and Clay will be happy there."

"Mr. Matheson, ever since I was a little girl, this has hung by my bedside." She pulled the blanket from the object it covered to reveal a framed piece of embroidery.

Boyd Matheson was obviously impressed by what he saw. He gently took the item that Laurel handed to him. "Whoever did this sure could use a needle and thread." He read aloud the words done in needlework. " 'The Lord is my shepherd. I shall not want. Psalm Twenty-three.' "

"My mother made it, a long time ago. I was seven when my parents died."

"This is something very special, Miss Remick. You'll want to . . ."

While they were talking, Laurel had nervously folded the blanket. She took a few steps to her right and started to lay it on Matheson's bed, then hastily changed course and placed it on the small bedside table. She walked back toward the sheriff. "Mr. Matheson, it would be such a pleasure to me if you were to accept this as a gift. Please. You have done so much for this town." Laurel paused, then continued. "And you have done a lot for me. Please accept this gift."

"Miss Remick, I can't do that. You need to keep this needlework in the family—"

"I think of you as family, Mr. Matheson!" Laurel looked down at the floor, hastily crushing the tears that escaped her eyes. When she looked up again, the tears were gone, and the young woman even managed a smile. "I want to do more for you, but I know that I can't." She gestured nervously at the embroidery. "This has been a part of me. Now I want you to have it, always. Please, Mr. Matheson."

"Thank you, Miss Remick. I'll hang this on my wall. Psalm twenty-three is important to me. I've memorized it."

Laurel's face brightened. "So have I!"

"That doesn't surprise me." Matheson gave the woman a look of warmth and affection, then became self-conscious and tried to lighten the mood. "Most folks would probably be surprised to learn that I have memorized a Psalm. But then, a man with a bad cough like mine should spend as much time with the Good Book as he can."

Laurel, sensing his unease, laughed with the sheriff. The laughter was followed by an awkward moment of silence. "Well, I guess I'd better be going." She looked about in a slightly confused manner, then retrieved the old blanket from the bedside table. "Uh, Grandfather needs me back at the store." She again looked around, this time for no apparent reason. "Come on, Perkins."

Matheson followed them to the door. He had only planned to say good-bye but suddenly blurted out, "Miss Remick, thank you for the gift. I will look at that needle-work every morning that I have left on this earth and give thanks for the wonderful friends that I have."

Laurel looked directly into the sheriff's eyes and said softly, "I pray for you every day, Mr. Matheson." She paused as if preparing to say more but suddenly turned and left hastily.

Chapter Twenty-Five

A team of four horses pulled the box wagon of *Dr. Smiley's Medicine Show* down the main street of Gradyville. Two of Judge Cavanaugh's gang rode on each side of the wagon, firing guns into the air. Clint Smith sat in the driver's seat, holding the reins with one hand and waving to the crowd with the other. A banjo player sat beside him loudly strumming "Oh! Susanna."

It was early Saturday evening, and the boardwalks were filled with people. Clint stopped the wagon in the middle of the road close to Flynn's Restaurant, as his boss had instructed him to do a few hours earlier. That way, they could attract the families who had come into town for an evening of socializing along with the usual barflies, gamblers, and men out to get rid of their week's pay. The judge sure knew how to think like a politician, Smith mused to himself. Guess that's how he'll get to the governor's mansion.

164

The banjo player was good, and some people began to clap their hands and even dance around the wagon. Clint Smith stood up and waved his hat to the crowd. When the music stopped, he shouted out loudly, "Guess I should apologize to you gents. Some of you probably thought this was a real medicine show, complete with dancing girls. Instead, all you get is some dull fella asking you to vote for him."

The crowd had been put into a festive mood, and Clint's joke received appreciative laughter. "But, at least, I'm a different kind of politician. You see, I believe in telling the truth." Clint shrugged his shoulders in a comical manner, as the crowd responded with more laughter. "I got a promise to keep, and I intend to do it real soon. But first, I would sure like to hear some more sounds out of that banjo. How about you good people?"

The crowd cheered, and the music resumed. Folks once again started to clap their hands, dance, and sing. Most people noticed Boyd Matheson and his deputy standing on the boardwalk across from the restaurant but paid them little heed.

"That promise he's talking about." Adams spoke in a low voice to his boss. "It must be about Judge Cavanaugh making an appearance. I'll bet Cavanaugh is in that wagon."

"Maybe," the sheriff replied as he nodded quickly to both Hank and Orin Mellor. The two men had taken position at opposite ends of the crowd, ready to enforce order if the need arose.

More and more people joined in the frivolity, clapping their hands, singing, and dancing around the wagon. Clay Adams spotted Laurel across the street on the other boardwalk. They exchanged worried glances.

"This medicine show thing seems to be working well for Smith." Clay couldn't bring himself to look directly at Matheson. "Uh, you know, maybe you should try something like this."

"Maybe I should. Can you play the banjo?"

Adams guffawed in spite of himself and looked once again at his fiancée. Laurel still looked worried, but she also looked thoughtful. Clay was certain that the woman was plotting to do some similar hoorahing for Boyd Matheson. After all, Laurel was the best piano player in Gradyville.

But a piano couldn't be toted around like a banjo. Would she try to put on a rally of some kind inside the church, maybe after the evening service the following night? Of course, there was also a new piano at the Silver Creek Saloon. Clay Adams thought about that for a moment, then shook his head. "Wouldn't put it past her," he whispered to himself.

Clay's eyes shifted to the merriment going on in the street, but his mind wandered to the very strange relationship between Laurel and Boyd Matheson. He thought about Laurel's remarks concerning trails and wondered if she would have preferred to travel with Boyd had that choice been given to her. Of course, all of that was no never-mind. The sheriff knew he was a dying man and wouldn't let himself become a burden to Laurel or anyone else.

Clay wondered if he could act as fine if he were the dying man. He hoped so and realized that he had hit on the most important question of all. Was he a complaining man always wanting better, or was he a man like Boyd Matheson, a man who appreciated what he had and tried to do right?

The banjo playing stopped, and people applauded. Clint Smith once again waved his hat to the crowd. "I can't play the banjo, but I do have an instrument here that I'm pretty good at." He reached back into the wagon and pulled out a Henry rifle. "Don't worry, folks, nobody's gonna get hurt. Unlike some of the lawdogs in this town, I don't believe in hurting innocent people."

There was a large burst of laughter. But Matheson noticed that it was fueled by about six of Smith's cronies who were scattered throughout the crowd, four of them on horseback. As the laughter subsided, a large number of eyes darted in the direction of the lawmen, but they gave no response at all.

"Like I said before, I believe in keeping promises, and that's what I'm doing right now!" Smith fired the Henry into the air, the banjo player strummed a few notes, and Smith fired the rifle a second time.

Judge Cavanaugh, who had been hiding in a forested area behind Flynn's Restaurant, had no trouble hearing his cue. He rode onto the main street immediately after Clint Smith had fired for the second time.

There were several gasps from the crowd. One lady shouted, "That's him—Judge Cavanaugh!" Clay Adams tensed as Boyd Matheson held up a palm in a sign of caution. "There are women and kids all over the place," Matheson whispered. "We may have to let Cavanaugh go and then track him."

Cavanaugh reared his white horse up on its hind legs and waved to the crowd. Clint Smith noted that his boss, for all his strange behavior, was an excellent horseman.

"That's right, madam! I am Judge Lewis Rutherford Cavanaugh. I have been called the Robin Hood of the West because I don't believe that rich men should be able to hire thugs to do their bidding and call them lawmen. On Monday, you folks will have a chance to help me make Gradyville a better place to live. Vote for Clint Smith as sheriff. And now, if you'll excuse me, I'll bid you all a very pleasant good night."

The judge had just lightly raked his spurs against the white horse when a shot was heard from the sheriff's office. A few women screamed, and more shots could be heard as the four men on horseback began to fire into the air and ride between the two boardwalks, making it difficult to pursue Judge Cavanaugh.

Boyd Matheson signaled the Mellors to stay where they were and watch the crowd. Matheson's chest tightened as he and Clay Adams ran toward the sheriff's office.

Chapter Twenty-Six

Ezra Johnstone received a surprise as he stepped into the sheriff's office. Reverend Stubby was sitting at the desk, reading his Bible. The pastor looked up and gave the ranch owner a pleasant smile. "Good evening, Ezra."

"Evening, Reverend." Ezra approached the desk with determination. Tonight he would free his boy. If the man blocking Zack's freedom was a preacher, well, that didn't change anything.

"Sorta surprised to see you here." Ezra tried to sound casual.

Reverend Stubby nodded his head. "It's going to be a busy night. Boyd wants both of the Mellors out patrolling the streets. Orin's wife and kids are staying at the stable tonight, and—"

Ezra Johnstone suddenly exploded. "So, he leaves my boy's life in the hands of some half-pint who—"

169

The pastor continued to smile but said nothing. Ezra checked his outburst. "Sorry, Reverend. It's just that . . ."

"Forget it, Ezra. You've been walking in a very desolate valley. I know that, and if I can be of any help at all to you and your family, just let me know."

The ranch owner felt a pang of guilt but only for a moment. "Right now, all I need is to see my son."

"Of course, but first—"

Ezra waved his hands in what he hoped looked like a friendly gesture. "I know, Reverend, you have to check me out. You can see that I'm not carrying a gun."

"If you could—"

"You need me to take off my boots." Ezra sat down on a chair in front of the desk, as the clergyman got up and walked around to where he could inspect the boots.

"I'm sorry about this, Ezra."

"Don't worry, Reverend. After all, no man is above the law." The rancher bent over as if getting ready to remove a boot.

"Thanks for being so—" The clergyman stopped speaking as Ezra Johnstone whipped a small pistol from his boot and pointed it at him.

"You get the jail keys real quick, Reverend, then free my boy." The rancher spoke as he stood up.

"Ezra, I've known you for a long time. You'd never pull that trigger."

"Wrong, Reverend. You don't know me at all, because I don't even know myself anymore. I hate the man I've become. Because of me two good lads are dead. I'm heading for the deepest hole in perdition—where I belong. But first my son gets out of prison. I won't let him get butchered in a crossfire. Now, you get the keys."

"Ezra—"

"Move!" The rancher pointed the gun closer to Reverend Stubby's head. The clergyman reluctantly retrieved the keys from the desk where he had been sitting and walked through the door that led to the jail area. Ezra remained directly behind him, gun in hand.

"Father!" Zack Johnstone put down his book and bolted from the cot inside his cell. He could tell from the expression on Reverend Stubby's face that something was very wrong. Only after getting to his feet did he see the small gun in his father's hand.

"What?!" Zack's voice exploded with shock.

"Be quiet, boy."

Zack looked incredulous. "I never thought I'd see you pointing a gun at the pastor."

"Yeah, well, I never thought I'd see you in jail right beside a killer you tried to help escape after he held up the bank." Ezra nodded toward Russ Cavanaugh. "Everyone, keep quiet." The rancher stepped quickly to the back door of the building, opened it, and in a loud whisper declared, "All's clear."

Darby moved quickly inside, accompanied by another one of Judge Cavanaugh's henchmen. Both men had their guns drawn. "Thank you, Mr. Johnstone," Darby said with mock politeness. "Colson and me won't be stayin' long, but we expect you folks to be mighty cooperative with us while we're here."

Reverend Stubby noticed the strange contrast between the two outlaws. Darby was heavyset, over six feet, his entire body oozing strength. Colson was about average height, with skin that seemed to hang on him. He appeared to be a man who had lost a lot of weight because of disease. His face was pockmarked, and his eyes looked confused and desperate.

"My father sent you!" There was a childlike excitement in Russ Cavanaugh's voice. "You're here to free me!"

"That's right, Russ. You're daddy is sure takin' care of you." Darby laughed at his own remark, but no one except Colson understood why. Darby then turned toward the man holding the keys. "You must be the preacher, the one they call Stubby?"

"That's right."

"Open that cell, and turn Zack loose."

"Let me out first!" Russ yelled. "Be careful of Zack, he's—"

"Quiet, sonny!" Darby snapped his head back to Russ. "I'll get to you in good time." He turned back to Reverend Stubby. "Okay, preacher man, do what I told you."

The pastor opened the jail cell, but Zack Johnstone stood resolutely. "I'm staying where I am, thank you. Kindly close the door."

"Don't be a fool, Zack!" Ezra pleaded, throwing both of his arms toward his son. The small pistol was still in Ezra's right hand. "Run. You could get killed when they break Russ out!"

Zack gave a short, unpleasant laugh. "Looks like they're going to break him out right now. I'll have the place to myself for a while." Zack looked into the adjoining cell and laughed again. "To be perfectly honest, I'm looking forward to the solitude."

"The solitude of the grave is what you'll have!" Ezra shouted. "Don't you see? Matheson needs a scapegoat. Someone to blame for—"

"You've been talking with Clint Smith, haven't you, Father?"

The question obviously stunned Ezra Johnstone. He looked down at the floor, then quickly looked back up. "Yes, I've talked with him some. What about it?"

"Clint's been in here quite a bit, jawing with Russ." Zack's voice became accusatory. "That man's smooth when it comes to words, but he's a total stranger to truth. Never thought you'd be conned by the likes of him, Father."

"That's enough!" Darby stomped toward Zack and gave him two hard shoves to get him outside of the cell. He then tripped the young man, who ended up on the floor, lying at his father's feet. "You see, sonny, you're goin' to die while pullin' an escape," Darby said. "Can't very well shoot you in the cell."

"What!" Ezra Johnstone started to point his gun at Darby, but the gunman smashed his revolver against the side of the old man's head. Ezra dropped to the floor as Colson squealed with delight.

"Ezra!" Reverend Steuben dropped the jail keys and crouched over the injured rancher. Zack got onto his knees and scampered to his father's side.

Darby grabbed Ezra's pistol from where it had dropped on the floor, then picked up the keys and let Russ out of jail. "Everybody, do what you're told!" There was an element of desperation in the gunman's voice as he stuffed the small pistol into his gun belt. Why had he made that comment about killing Zack? He couldn't fire a gun until Judge Cavanaugh rode off. He'd have to rely on brutality and fear to keep the situation under control. Darby pointed his gun at the old man lying on the floor. "Get him up, and get him into the office. Now!"

Zack and Reverend Steuben helped Ezra to his feet and began to walk him slowly into the office. The two gunmen and the just-released prisoner followed closely behind them. "Thanks for freeing me, men."

"You're surely welcome." Those were the first words Colson had spoken since entering the jail area.

As the group moved into the office, Russ hurried to the desk and located his gun and holster in the third drawer that he opened. He strapped on the weapon, then declared in a bombastic voice, "Sure feels good having this back on. Felt naked without it."

A wide grin spread across Russ Cavanaugh's face. He didn't notice that his father's two henchmen did not appear all that amused.

"You and Colson keep an eye on those three." Darby looked at Russ as he motioned toward Reverend Steuben and Zack Johnstone, who had Ezra lying on a cot behind the desk. Zack held a bandanna against his father's head in an attempt to stop the bleeding.

Darby moved quickly to the door of the sheriff's office, opened it, and peered outside. "We won't have long to wait. Russ, that papa of yours is riding a white horse right up to a crowd of happy folks. Quite a show going on out there."

Russ laughed with astonishment. He once again sounded like a small boy. "Father is here! Well, great, yes, that's really great, but what do you mean by 'wait'? Wait for what?"

Darby ignored the question, keeping his eyes on the show. "The judge is getting ready to ride out!" Darby closed the door, ran to the cot, and fired a bullet into Ezra Johnstone. A powerful tremor of shock and grief passed through Zack. He was unable to take in what he had just witnessed.

Colson squealed with excitement. "Let me kill this one!" He pointed his gun toward Russ Cavanaugh.

"You're not supposed to kill me!" Russ gripped the six-shooter that was in his hand.

Darby smiled mockingly at Russ Cavanaugh. He also had a gun in his right hand and knew he could use it better than the fool kid he was facing. "You're half right. We weren't supposed to do it til later. Colson just changed that. Guess both of us are being a mite too talkative tonight—we'll have to kill you now."

Zack Johnstone had been temporarily paralyzed by his father's murder. The two outlaws had paid no heed to the small pastor, not thinking him to be a threat. Reverend Steuben took advantage of their stupidity. He tackled Darby, and the two men went down before Darby could fire his gun. Stubby hit the gunman with a barrage of hard punches to the head. Darby let go of his gun as he fought to maintain consciousness.

Colson raised his Remington but couldn't get a clean shot at the pastor. It was almost too late when he saw Zack Johnstone coming at him. The gunman fired at the fast-moving blur, and Zack whirled, staggered, then collided with the desk before flopping onto the floor. Colson's happy squeal stopped abruptly as he saw Reverend Stubby on his feet, holding Darby's Colt .44. Colson attempted a shot but didn't have the time to squeeze the trigger of his Remington before the pastor fired the .44. Colson squealed for the last time as he plunged into eternity.

As Reverend Stubby scrambled to help Zack, he looked about for Russ Cavanaugh.

But the outlaw was gone.

Chapter Twenty-Seven

Judge Lewis Rutherford Cavanaugh turned his white horse as the cheers from the crowd almost covered the gunshots that came from the sheriff's office. Boyd Matheson and Clay Adams were running toward the office, and the crowd followed them. But it was unclear why so many people were running along the boardwalks. Some of them seemed to be following the fabled Judge Cavanaugh as he rode out of Gradyville.

One voice in the crowd shouted, "Things will be a lot better when your man is in charge of law and order, Judge!"

Judge Cavanaugh waved to the crowd and received some cheers. He had originally planned to gallop out of town but chose instead to prance his horse. The law already had plenty on their hands, and it was unlikely that they'd risk a shot with so many folks, including women and children, around. Besides, Judge Lewis Rutherford Cavanaugh was savoring this moment.

A figure ran out of the sheriff's office to the middle of the street, firing a gun into the air. As Judge Cavanaugh neared the figure, his first thought was to spur his horse and ride quickly out of town. But he immediately rejected that notion. A fast exit now would be humiliating; a future governor doesn't run from his own son.

Judge Cavanaugh stopped his horse and spoke in a loud, hearty voice, trying to maintain the festive mood, which had not been completely shattered by the gunshots. "Russ, good to see you, boy!"

Russ Cavanaugh laughed, gripped his gun, and said nothing. He was watching the crowd, which was now beginning to fill both boardwalks near the sheriff's office.

Russ was waiting until he had a large audience. His father sensed that and didn't like it. "Get on a horse, son. Let's get out of here."

"What for, Judge? So that you can kill me once we get out of town?"

Exclamations of shock moved through the crowd, mixed with uneasy laughter. Clint Smith had jumped off the wagon and was now standing among the bystanders, trying to come up with a plan to silence Russ.

Matheson stopped outside of the office while Clay darted in and emerged less than a minute later carrying a Winchester. Both men nodded to Doc Evans as he ran up to them, his black bag in hand.

"Just got back into town." Evans was breathing hard as he spoke. "Delivered a baby at the McNelly Ranch. Sounds like you could use me."

Russ' voice continued to thunder. "No, Judge, I don't think you'd kill me. That's not your way. You'd arrange for someone else to do your dirty work."

Matheson's attention was focused primarily on the scene in the middle of the street. His deputy hurriedly replied to the doctor. "I was just inside and got a quick look. Things are under control, but it's bad. We've got two men dead and another, Zack Johnstone, seriously hurt. Reverend Stubby is tying up an unconscious owl-hoot. He can help you with Zack."

Doc Evans nodded and ran into the sheriff's office as the two lawmen walked to the edge of the boardwalk. They were standing directly across from Clint Smith. "Think we should try to arrest the judge and Russ right now?" Clay asked.

"No," the sheriff replied. "For once, I think Russ Cavanaugh may have something worthwhile to say. Let's give him his ground."

Judge Cavanaugh had been pretending to laugh. He tried to sound amused as he shouted to the crowd. "That boy of mine has always had a crazy sense of humor. Why, I remember the time—"

"I'm not joking, Judge!" Russ shouted louder than his father. "Or should I call you *Graham Ellison*?"

Even in the poor lighting from the oil lamps hanging over the boardwalks, people could see Judge Cavanaugh's face twitch with worry. Clint Smith also looked tense. The gunman thought about making a run for it but decided against it. This could still turn out in his favor.

"You folks have heard of Graham Ellison, haven't

you? The writer who turns out all those thrilling tales about Judge Cavanaugh." Russ pointed his gun almost casually at his father. "Well, that's him, Graham Ellison. Yeah, the great Judge Lewis Rutherford Cavanaugh spends his days making up fables about himself!"

Clint Smith looked about as laughter began to erupt at several places in the crowd. "That's not true!" he shouted. "He's lying!"

"Clint Smith sure knows a lot about lying." Russ' eyes were moist. He seemed to be having fun and suffering a horrible torment at the same time. "Why not tell folks your real name, Clint? Maybe you can't remember it. Can you remember the names of the men you bragged to me about killing, like Walter Jarrett?"

That revelation threw a brief silence over the crowd, which Laurel Remick shattered. "This chapter doesn't seem to be going very well for you, Mr. Graham Ellison!" she yelled out. "Maybe you'd better rewrite it!"

Loud, mocking laughter surrounded Judge Cavanaugh. Clint Smith looked at the young woman who stood a few feet from him. It was the same gal who had given him trouble when he spoke in the church. Now she was causing trouble again, plenty of trouble. Smith spotted the gang members who had ridden into town with him, now riding off. Instead of sitting behind the sheriff's desk, as was the plan, Clint Smith knew that he could soon be sitting in jail awaiting trial for Jarrett's murder. He had to make a move fast. But he had to be careful; the sheriff's eyes were frequently darting in his direction.

"The lady is right, Judge!" a male voice shouted from the crowd. "Maybe you should jump up onto a roof and disappear into the night, like Robin Hood!"

The laughter increased. The worried look on Judge Cavanaugh's face transitioned into horror. People were mocking him, and he was helpless to do anything about it.

"Maybe the title of his next book should be *Judge Cavanaugh's Last Stand.*" As he spoke, Russ Cavanaugh fired a bullet into his father's chest.

Shouts and screams blared from the crowd as the judge tumbled from his white horse.

"Throw down your gun, Russ!" Matheson shouted as he drew his weapon.

Russ Cavanaugh did not obey the order. Ignoring the lawmen, he ran toward his father's twitching body. Russ intended to put another bullet into the Robin Hood of Arizona. He never even saw Clay Adams' fist coming at him. He only felt an explosion inside his head as he plunged to the ground.

Adams grabbed the young man's gun and ran to check on the older Cavanaugh. "He's alive, but barely!" the deputy shouted. "We'd better get him inside the office. Doc Evans can look at him after taking care of Zack."

"Leave him there!" Matheson's voice resounded with a tension and alarm that Clay Adams hadn't heard before.

"Wha—"

"We've got other things to do." As the sheriff spoke, he saw Clint Smith push Harold Flynn away from the entrance to his own restaurant. Smith had a gun in one hand, and with the other he grabbed Laurel Remick and forced her inside Flynn's Restaurant. He had taken her hostage.

Chapter Twenty-Eight

The main street of Gradyville was overwhelmed by confusion. Some people had been frightened by the shooting of Judge Cavanaugh and were running off. Mothers were rounding up their children and getting them away from the violence. There were a large number of drunks, some of whom were shouting out phrases of angry nonsense while others were laughing over the haymaker Clay Adams had given Russ Cavanaugh. Only a handful of people seemed to have noticed Clint Smith forcing Laurel Remick into the restaurant, and they didn't seem to understand what was happening.

Boyd Matheson understood completely. The man who called himself Clint Smith had been exposed as a fraud and a killer. He knew that a very bitter Russ Cavanaugh would testify against him in court and send

183

him to the gallows. Smith's only hope was to get far away from Gradyville, and Laurel Remick was his ticket.

Hank and Orin Mellor approached the two lawmen. Both men had been keeping an eye on the opposite boardwalk. "Orin, you were close to the restaurant—"

Orin hastily nodded his head. He understood the lawman's question before it was asked. "Smith is inside the restaurant with the girl. Talked with Harold Flynn. No one else in there, just Smith and the Remick girl."

"What!?" Clay Adams shouted. His face went pale.

Matheson grabbed his deputy's right shoulder. "We're going to get Laurel back—safe! But to do that, I need you to be a lawman, not some crazy school kid. Understand that?"

"I got it," Adams replied in a steady monotone. "You can count on me."

Matheson quickly turned his attention to the two Mellors. "Hank, get Russ Cavanaugh back inside and in jail. If the judge is still alive, get him into the office, where Doc Evans can look at him. Orin, clear the boardwalks, get people out of here. There's a curfew now in effect. When you're finished, both of you join up with Clay and me."

"Where?" Orin shot back.

"As soon as the boardwalks clear, we're going to be behind that wagon, the one Clint Smith rode in on." Matheson pointed in the direction of the box wagon. "The one with *Dr. Smiley's Medicine Show* painted on it."

The contrast between *Dr. Smiley's Medicine Show* and the grim situation registered in each man's mind, but no one commented on it. Orin hopped off the boardwalk and fired a pistol into the air. "Everybody, go home! We got us a curfew. If you don't get out soon, you'll be in jail! I mean it. Vamoose! This town's closin' down for the night."

A few drunks shouted words of defiance, but most people seemed willing enough to do what they were told. Hank Mellor's naturally loud voice could be heard above the footsteps and chattering as people headed for home. "Judge Cavanaugh's dead or close enough to it that it don't make no never mind. I'll get the fool kid into jail." Hank scrambled over to Russ Cavanaugh, who was now sitting up, caressing his jaw.

"As soon as the crowd is gone, we'll make a run for the wagon." Matheson spoke in a soft voice to his deputy. "Smith will take a few shots at us—I hope."

"What do you mean?"

"We need to keep Clint Smith very busy. That hard case is smart, and he's holding all the good cards. Harold Flynn brags to everyone about his guns. Smith knows that there are plenty of weapons and ammo for him to use in those rooms the Flynns live in. And he's inside a restaurant; plenty of food and drink. He could hold out for days and force us to bargain with him for Laurel."

"Do you think he'd try to—"

"Don't even mention that!" Matheson snapped. "We're not going to give him the chance."

"How—"

Matheson looked over the town. The boardwalks were now empty except for a few drunks staggering

around and yelling about their rights. Orin Mellor
looked ready to give up on them. Matheson didn't care
if he did.

"We're making a run for the wagon," the sheriff said,
"then we're going to rush Smith."

"Shouldn't we come at him from two different
sides?" Adams looked confused and worried.

"That's not what I have in mind." For the moment,
Matheson couldn't explain any further.

Hank Mellor came running out of the sheriff's office.
"Cavanaugh kid's back in jail. Doc Evans and the reverend are workin' on Zack—they think he'll make it."

"Good. It's time we pay a visit to 'Dr. Smiley.' With
luck, we'll draw fire from Smith when we get in range
of Flynn's. We can send a few shots in the direction of
the restaurant, but don't fire directly at Smith."

"Why?" Hank asked.

"We need to get an idea of where Laurel is inside
that restaurant. A stray bullet could find her. Hank, right
now that shotgun of yours is only for decoration. Use
your pistol, and only use it with purpose when we find
out where the girl is." Matheson gave Clay Adams a re-
assuring smile. "That young lady is engaged to a lawman. I reckon she'll know what we're up to and give us
some help. Let's go!"

The three men ran toward the wagon. As they moved
into range of Flynn's Restaurant, shots came at them,
spraying dust near their boots. As Matheson instructed,
the men fired back but purposely fired wide.

Boyd Matheson reached the wagon first. He leaned
against it and began to cough.

"You okay?" The concern in Clay Adams' voice was too intense. Matheson again suspected that Laurel had told the deputy about his condition. Maybe that was for the best. It might make it easier for Clay to go along with his plan.

"Probably got some dust in his throat—" As Hank spoke, there were more shots from the restaurant. Orin Mellor ran behind the wagon, accompanied by Beau Kibler.

When he saw the reporter, Matheson laughed, the laugh turning into a slight cough as the lawman spoke. "Beau, you're wearing your gun on your hip, and you're carrying that notebook and pencil in your hands."

"Sorry, Sheriff, I—"

"There's nothing to be sorry for." Matheson's voice was now more firm. "Every man uses the weapon he knows best. That pencil of yours can be pretty powerful at times."

"I'm afraid this isn't one of those times." Kibler looked sheepish.

"No, guess not, but keep doing what you do best." Matheson turned to his deputy. "Now, you're going to do what you do better than anyone in this town, me in-cluded."

"What—"

"Use that Winchester of yours." Matheson pointed at the weapon in his deputy's hand, then shouted toward the restaurant. "Turn the girl loose, Smith. Then follow her with your hands held high."

The forced laugh of a desperate man came from the restaurant; then, as Matheson expected, Clint Smith yelled back in defiance. "You want to get the girl back, you're going to do just what I say, Matheson. Adams, you tell that boss of yours to act smart, or you'll never see your girl again!"

"Don't do it, Clay! Don't bargain with a devil!" Laurel Remick's words were followed by several loud barks.

"Laurel's on the far left side of the restaurant," Matheson said in a loud whisper. "Perkins is with her. Always liked that mutt. Way I see it, now we got two hostages to rescue."

"But how?" Adams didn't quite succeed in keeping the anxiety out of his voice.

"Smith is pretty shaken up. Before he has a chance to settle, I'm going to rush him, draw him out, make him lean out that window a bit. When he does, you'll be ready with the Winchester."

"You can't do that, Boyd!" Beau Kibler proclaimed in a loud whisper. "It would be suicide!"

"Beau, I told you to stick with your pencil." Matheson turned to his deputy, whose face was ashen with myriad emotions sweeping across it. "You be ready with that Winchester, okay?"

Clay Adams could only nod his head.

Matheson suddenly experienced a terror he had never known before. The former gunfighter had plunged himself into plenty of dangerous situations, but there had always been a decent chance of coming out of it alive. Not much hope of that here. But Matheson knew that there was only one way to free Laurel, and he needed to do it.

The lawman closed his eyes in a brief, silent prayer. When he opened them, the terror was still inside him, but it was under control.

Boyd Matheson ran toward the restaurant. He fired two shots toward the right side of the window. Clint Smith returned fire, and Matheson felt a sharp, burning pain in one side. He dropped to the ground, rolled in the opposite direction of the restaurant, then, somehow, buoyed back onto his feet. He could see Clint Smith peeking at him from a corner of the window. The lawman tried to yell out at the outlaw, but a vicious cough racked his body.

Clint Smith laughed bitterly, then shouted from his cover, "Not feeling so good, Sheriff? Maybe you need to take a nap." He fired at the lawman, but Matheson was now standing in front of the boardwalk opposite the restaurant, and Smith would only allow a fraction of his body to be exposed by the window. The shot went wide.

Matheson's coughing stopped, and he actually sounded lighthearted as he shouted back. "Smith, or whatever your real name is, I may have a bad cough and a bullet inside me, but I could still lick you in anything close to a fair fight."

Boyd Matheson twirled his Colt, then dropped it into his holster. He stood ramrod tall, his posture not betraying the terrible burn that was spreading through his body. "Come out into the street! Show this town what a brave man you are!" Matheson gave a mocking laugh. "I say you haven't got the sand to face a wounded man eye to eye. You're a coward! You killed Jarrett while he lay unconscious in the doctor's office. Bet you didn't kill Joel Hogan and Tommy Skerrit in a fair fight. You're yellow—"

A wild rage flamed from the hired gun's eyes as he leaned out the window and fired twice at Matheson. That rage turned to shock, and then Clint Smith's face vanished with a good portion of his head. Clay Adams' shot had been perfect.

Matheson staggered and collapsed. He wasn't sure if one or both of Smith's bullets had found him, but he reckoned that it didn't make too much difference. A wave of nausea came over the lawman; through it he could hear Perkins barking as Clay and Laurel rushed together and then ran toward him. Even in his pain, Matheson could smile. The lawman could tell that everything was fine by the way Perkins barked. Those were happy yaps coming from the mongrel.

"Mr. Matheson!" Laurel dropped to her knees and grasped Matheson's right hand, caressing it gently. Perkins was on one side of her. On her other side Clay Adams crouched down.

"You just take it easy," Clay said anxiously. "Beau has gone for Doc Evans."

"That was a good shot, Deputy," Matheson replied. "You're going to make this town a fine sheriff."

Boyd Matheson shifted his gaze to Laurel. "I have that embroidery you gave me, hanging on my wall. I surely appreciate the gift. But I want you to take it back. It's . . ." Matheson paused for a moment as the pain and dizziness took a fast surge and then diminished some. "It's an heirloom. You and Clay should have it."

"The important thing is the Psalm itself," the young woman replied hastily. "You told me that you had memorized Psalm Twenty-three, Mr. Matheson. Why don't we say it together?"

Perspiration now covered the sheriff's face. His voice became faint. "I . . . I don't think I can. . . ."

Laurel gripped Matheson's hand harder, as if trying to keep his soul on earth. "I'll say it for you, Mr. Matheson. 'The Lord is my shepherd; I shall not want.' "

Matheson's eyes closed, and a slight smile formed on his lips. Laurel Remick knew that the words were bringing him comfort. " 'He maketh me to lie down in green pastures. . . .' "

Laurel continued to recite the Psalm, even after Boyd Matheson's hand went limp. " 'Surely goodness and mercy shall follow me all the days of my life, and I will dwell in the house of the Lord forever.' "

She gently let go of the hand and then turned into her fiancé's embrace. They wept together.

Chapter Twenty-Nine

Fourteen months later

Laurel held Matheson in her arms, made a funny face at him, then lifted the infant into the air. "Clay Matheson Adams," she said, as the baby flailed his arms and legs about happily. "You can't go wrong with a name like that."

The young mother placed Clay against her right shoulder, carried him to his cradle, and gently laid him in it. "But right now you need to get some sleep. Otherwise, you'll get all crabby and cry a lot." She tickled his tummy with one finger. "We want to keep you a happy boy."

Laurel sang quietly to the child while rocking his cradle. As the baby fell asleep, Laurel realized that she was singing a hymn that had been sung at Boyd Matheson's funeral.

* * *

She had done what Matheson had instructed. Only a few hours after Boyd Matheson died, Laurel went to the sheriff's room and took the needlework down from his wall. She was comforted in knowing that on the very morning of his death, he had awakened with the quote from the twenty-third Psalm being one of the very first things he saw. Laurel wondered if Boyd Matheson had thought of her at all on that last morning of his life. She thought about the awkward conversation the two of them had stumbled through on the afternoon she brought the needlework to him. Laurel hadn't known it would be the last private conversation they ever had together. How could she have? Laurel wished that she had said more, but what could she have said?

She hadn't wanted to leave immediately. She had stayed in the room for a while, not saying anything, not even thinking much. Then she quietly left.

Laurel had vowed that she would not cry at Boyd Matheson's funeral. After all, she would be sitting in front of the church at the piano. People should be paying attention to what the pastor said and to the words of the hymns. They shouldn't even notice the pianist.

The young woman had kept that vow. Boyd Matheson had loved her—she knew that now—but he had never let emotion interfere with what was for the best. She would do no less.

Still, there was one more thing she had to do for Boyd. As the service ended, Laurel rose from the piano and walked to the open coffin. In her hand was the needlework that had hung briefly on Matheson's wall.

She had taken it from its frame and rolled it into a neat cylinder, and now she tucked it into the lawman's motionless hand. Then, employing all the will she had, the young woman tried to give Boyd Matheson one of those mischievous smiles she knew he loved so much, but she couldn't quite bring it off.

She felt the pastor's hand on her arm. "Boyd is smiling right now because you tried to" came the whisper. She quickly turned away before the coffin was closed.

Clay Matheson Adams was asleep. Laurel bent over and petted Perkins, who was lying beside her and gazing up intently as if reading the young woman's mind. "I know you miss him too."

She got up from the chair and retrieved a sewing basket. "Mr. Matheson was right about that needlework," she whispered to the dog. "It was a family heirloom, but that heirloom is where it belongs now."

She once again sat down in the chair beside the cradle. Placing the sewing basket beside the chair, Laurel gave Perkins a broad smile. "It's time I get busy making some new family heirlooms."

Chapter Thirty

Reverend Steuben walked into the sheriff's office and dropped a book onto the sheriff's desk. Clay Adams looked up, happy for a distraction from his paperwork.

"I read it cover to cover last night," Reverend Stubby said. "I know you and Laurel will enjoy it."

Adams smiled as he read out loud from the cover: "*Boyd Matheson: Gunfighter and Lawman* by Beau Kibler."

"Boyd told me quite a few things about himself," the pastor said. "I hope Boyd wouldn't feel that I was breaking a confidence by passing it all on to Beau. But I'm tired of outlaws and other riffraff being made into heroes. It's time a real hero got due recognition."

Sheriff Clay Adams nodded his head. "Thanks for lending us the book. We'll get it back to you right quick."

"Keep it." The pastor smiled as he spoke. "I have

195

three other copies. Two copies of *Boyd Matheson: Gun-fighter and Lawman* will be the main attraction when the new library opens tomorrow."

Clay Adams tried to stifle a laugh.

Reverend Stubby shrugged his shoulders in a comical manner. "Okay, so the new Gradyville Public Library will consist of four shelves in a corner of Remick's General Store. It's a start!"

"You're right, Reverend, sorry. I know that Laurel is really looking forward to running the whole thing. A library, even a small one, is a step forward for this town."

Reverend Steuben looked a bit uneasy. "Speaking of the future of the town, I understand that we are losing a deputy sheriff."

Clay missed the tension in the pastor's remark. "Yeah, Ray made a fine deputy, but the man has an itchy foot—went and got himself a fancy new position as a railroad detective."

"I know just the man to take his place." The pastor's smile was a bit forced.

"Who?"

"Zack Johnstone."

Clay's chin dropped in surprise. "Zack just got back into town from doing jail time!"

"That's right, and he's looking for a job."

"Why would he need a job?" Clay's voice was defiant. He wanted no part of the mayor's suggestion. "He's got that huge spread to take care of."

"The huge spread is doing just fine without him." Reverend Stubby began speaking more aggressively.

"Besides, Zack doesn't want to be a rancher. He wants to be a lawman. He made some stupid mistakes and hurt a lot of people. He's done his time for it, and now he wants to start doing some good. The way I see it, being your deputy is just what he needs right now, and, believe me, Clay, you won't regret it. Zack will be the best deputy you could ever ask for."

The sheriff shook his head. "I understand what you are saying, Reverend, and I do like Zack, but, no, I can't pin a badge on a man who just got out of jail."

Reverend Stubby was silent for a moment; then he looked at the book on the sheriff's desk. "That's a good drawing of Boyd on the cover, don't you think?"

Clay was not expecting the sudden diversion. "Uh, yes."

"You know, I can remember when Boyd Matheson appointed a very troubled young man to be his deputy. A young man who needed some guidance and the opportunity to prove that he could be more than a hired gun."

Adams started laughing and held up two hands as if in surrender. "Okay, okay. Boyd gave me a chance, so maybe I can at least talk to Zack about—"

"Wonderful!" the pastor cut in. "Right now, Zack is over at Remick's General Store, helping Cassius rearrange things for the library. We could go over there and help out a bit, then maybe you, Zack, and myself could have lunch together."

The sheriff stood up and continued to laugh as he retrieved his hat. "I know when I'm licked."

Reverend Stubby looked at the book cover and gave Boyd Matheson a quick salute. Then the two men left the office to meet with the next deputy sheriff of Gradyville.